The SWING of the GATE

When a midnight murder makes local head-lines, trainee reporter Alan Bishop finds him-self personally drawn into the story. For the prime suspect is his half-brother, Lennie.

Soon Sergeant Hendricks is on the case, digging and probing for a solution. His ques-tioning provokes in Alan a sequence of memories which takes him back to his coun-try childhood, to the shadowy figure of Aunt Val and to Uncle Ross, the man who taught him and Lennie how to use a gun.

The memory of a gate swings into focus in Alan's mind, and with it bitterness at the ac-cident which left him with a withered hand. Is his urge to protect his blood-relation the mo-tive force behind Alan's attempt to track Len-nie down and confront him before the police can find him; or is it a surging hatred?

Roy Brown's new novel of mystery and sus-pense shows a remarkable psychological power and penetration. It is a worthy com-panion to his earlier books, FIND DEBBIE! and THE CAGE.

Other Novels by Roy Brown

The
SWING
of the
GATE

by Roy Brown

A CLARION BOOK
THE SEABURY PRESS
NEW YORK

The Seabury Press, 815 Second Ave, New York, NY 10017

Library of Congress Cataloging in Publication Data

Brown, Roy.
   The swing of the gate.

   "A Clarion book."
   SUMMARY: A young reporter investigating the murder of a call girl,
uncovers evidence that casts suspicion on his own brother.
   [1. Mystery and detective stories]   I. Title.
PZ7.B81693SW   [Fic]   78-6422 ISBN 0-8164-3220-1

chapter 1

The little man in the witness box was guilty, of course. His fingers twitched on the oak ledge, grubby nails making scratching sounds in the brief silences.

Occasionally his eyes drifted up to the high gray windows, their preposterous innocence at last shifting in defeat; yet the gaze back still held the perky, defiant brightness of a fox cornered among chickens.

The prosecuting counsel's brief evidently held nothing in it of the quality of mercy. "Yes, we all understand, Mr. Gimble, why you felt persecuted by the police. After all, as you have frequently protested, you were simply making your way peaceably home, perfectly sober, along High Street at three o'clock in the morning. The attaché case in your possession was one you had picked up a few minutes earlier in a men's room. I won't labor the point that the lavatory you mentioned is regularly locked at eleven o'clock at night.

"Now, at the time of your arrest you claimed to be on your way through an alley that you assumed was a short cut to the police station. The constable has told us that in your statement you expressed a fear that the case might contain an explosive device. Not an entirely unreasonable supposition, Mr. Gimble—we have all read of such things. Indeed in other circumstances I am sure the Court would applaud your courage and sense of duty . . ."

In what passed for the press gallery, Alan Bishop abandoned any attempt to take down a verbatim report. His short-

1

hand, anyway, was execrable. More than once he'd been tempted to dig out the little Grundig he always carried, but he'd been told that the judge had a horror of tape recorders. Well, this wasn't much of a case—which was probably why Bill Finch, the regular crime reporter on *The Clapham and Tooting Weekly,* had pushed off to cover a story more worthy of his expertise, leaving a mere trainee to cut his teeth in the local Crown Court.

Alan bit the thumb of his withered left hand and continued half listening to the young lawyer's labored hatchet job on the unfortunate Mr. Gimble. "And when you saw the patrol car turn the corner, how were you to know that it contained real policemen? You were being harried, weren't you Mr. Gimble, by imposters—those subversive enemies of the state who had, for political reasons we needn't go into, gone to the trouble of setting a time bomb in a locked toilet! I am sure, also, that the Court takes a sympathetic view of your claim that, when ultimately the case was found to contain stolen jewelry, this had been wilfully planted on you in a plot to tarnish your good name . . ."

Counsel for the defense struggled impatiently to his feet. "My Lord, *must* my client be subjected to this tedious display of histrionics?"

The judge removed his spectacles and glowered. "I think not! Mr. Humphreys, *do* get on. Surely even you must know that hanging, drawing and quartering is no longer regarded as a civilized method of dealing with prisoners."

"As your Lordship pleases . . ."

At the newspaper office, Alan found a deserted typewriter and one-handedly pecked out his copy. A couple of hundred words would do—the subeditor would cut it by half, anyway. The wrong half, as the other reporters always said.

Court had adjourned early, thank goodness. The jury had

scarcely needed to retire, but they had to fit in lunch somewhere. A simple phone call later would elicit the inevitable verdict and the sentence the judge handed out with it.

The reporters' room began to fill. It was almost twelve o'clock and whoever was around took a tea break. Somebody shoved a cup and saucer beside Alan on the desk. "You can do better than that, Bish. Get a move on. You're wanted on the murder case."

Trying to concentrate, Alan hardly heard. He was aware only of the usual office chatter: ribald exchanges, shop talk . . . Then the conversation turned to something new.

"I expect she asked for it."

"Oh, come on! Even a tart doesn't deserve *that*."

"Who says she was a tart?"

"What do you think she was doing out on the common at that time of night? Picking daisies?"

"Radio says she was found at seven this morning."

"Yeah, but later the pathologist reckoned she'd been done in hours before."

"*They* never know."

"What's it to us? The story will be colder than Maggie by the time we hit the street next Tuesday. Just our luck, being a weekly rag."

"They can always give it to young Bish. It'll take him six days to grind his way through the first quarter column."

"Not if he keeps his mind off the sexy bits!"

"What's the problem, Bish? Split another infinitive?"

Alan fumbled for his pipe. "Maggie . . . Maggie who?"

"Why the interest, Bish? Don't tell us *you've* been up to something with Maggie?"

"You know what they say about Bishops."

"And actresses!"

A slightly more serious voice somewhere said, "Maggie Jones . . . sounds like a girl in an old song."

3

Alan eventually extricated himself from the reporters' room and collected his motor bike from the yard at the back.

The sense of shock was still with him. Maggie Jones—it must be the same girl, surely—had shared a flat near the common with his half sister, Shirley. His impulse had been to ride straight over, offer sympathy, maybe some sort of help. Not, Alan thought ironically, that we Bishops formed much of a mutual aid society! And he didn't see Shirley very often, had rarely come across Maggie and wasn't sure that he wanted to be involved. The girls' apartment would probably be crawling with police, and his turning up there at this time of day would achieve nothing. Poor old Shirley, though. She'd been fond of Maggie. He'd call that evening when she'd most likely be alone.

And yet . . . he couldn't quite leave it there. He wanted to know more—wanted access to a radio.

Unable to explain this sudden sense of uneasiness, he skilfully navigated his Suzuki through the thickening traffic, heading for his room near Tooting Broadway. The examiners had insisted on only small modifications to the bike's controls, including a special clutch lever fitted to his right, adjacent to the front brake mechanism. They had decided, with some reservations, that Alan's damaged left hand had sufficient strength to grasp the nearside handlebar.

It was sheer folly, of course, climbing up those newly vacuumed stairs during the day. Alan sometimes felt that of all the rooms in the house *his* received the most conscientious attention from Mrs. Friday, his landlady. An opening of windows to let out pipe smoke, a flick at scattered ash, a long-suffering brushing of burned carpet—not to mention frequent sprays of furniture polish over any papers he had been careless enough to leave on his desk.

He plugged in the electric kettle, switched on the radio to a

London station, then threw a couple of tea bags into a stained cup while he was waiting for the kettle to sing.

The one o'clock news came on:

> ". . . body of a girl, identified as Maggie Jones, found strangled early this morning near the edge of Clapham Common. It has been established that death probably occurred around midnight. A woman walking her dog discovered the body just before seven this morning. A police spokesman said that a large-scale hunt for the killer is in progress, and an early arrest is expected . . ."

Alan impulsively turned off the radio. It was always a beacon to Mrs. Friday. She'd home in on it with the unerring sense of direction of a transcontinental missile.

He was right. There came a perfunctory knock, then entry. Mrs. Friday was large, bulky and blowsy with an air of friendliness which, on a bad day, made you prefer a bitter and mealy-mouthed hostility upon which to slam a door.

"Feeling under the weather?"

"What makes you say that?"

"You don't often pop home during the day."

"I've been in court all morning. Finished early. Thought I'd pop in for some papers."

"What about the murder, then?"

"Murder?"

"You haven't heard? Some little floozie out on the common. Maggie something—strangled. I suppose she asked for it. But, to be charitable, if we all got what we asked for the world wouldn't have a population problem would it?"

She giggled, flesh wobbling, eyes drifting about. Then, "Your girl friend rang."

"Sally!"

"You've got more than one?"

"When?"

"Just a few minutes ago. I don't know why she thought you'd be here."

Alan frowned. "Perhaps she tried the office and guessed . . . Is she calling back?"

"No. She wants you to call her—if you happened to drop in, she said."

"Thanks."

"Perhaps you'll be reporting the murder for your paper, eh? Good experience—hanging around the scene of the crime, waving your press card, looking for clues the police have overlooked. Must be an interesting life. My boy, Harry, wanted to be a reporter, you know. Instead of that he went to sea. What do your people think of your career?"

"My people?"

"You must have somebody. They don't seem to see much more of you than I do of my Harry."

Alan grinned. "There's always Christmas."

Mrs. Friday said, whimsically, "Last Christmas my Harry was in Rio de Janeiro—or so he said."

Alan didn't like using Mrs. Friday's phone. It was placed against a wall downstairs with a coin box attached, and there was a deceptive air of privacy which he didn't quite trust.

Normally it didn't matter. Why now? Sally could be calling about something trivial, but Alan doubted it. He was difficult to trace during the day, and if she'd used the school telephone she'd have had to go along to the secretary's office, abandoning or trying to hand over her classroom full of six-year-olds.

That strange feeling of unease came over him again as he dialed the number. Like a sweat, a cool, gentle sweat which he remembered all too well but . . . why *now?*

6

"May I speak to Miss Hendricks, please?"

"Just a minute."

Sally came breathlessly to the phone. "Alan!" Then a long pause.

"Something's wrong," he said.

"Well, I don't know . . . You haven't heard anything?"

"About what?"

"Lennie's out."

"From the hospital?" One of those stupid questions which came out like a gasp.

"Yes . . . I thought somebody might have told you."

"How do *you* know?" His voice was almost hostile.

Another pause. "Normally I could have slipped out and met you somewhere but we've got inspectors in . . . Are you free to talk?"

"You'd better do the talking."

"This may mean nothing . . . There's probably no connection. But Alan . . . that murder on the common . . ."

The sweat turned to balls of liquid—Alan felt them gather in the small of his back and shivered.

"Alan, are you still there?"

"Of course!"

"I got all this from Ted unofficially. He's on the case."

"That's a bit of a coincidence, isn't it?"

"Well, he *is* senior sergeant down there. He called me here at school—just as this inspector was watching me dish out paints. He wondered if I knew where you'd be—you'd just left your office."

"He called *there?*"

"Yes . . ."

"But why? Why me?"

Sally was trying to cope with Alan's reactions, as if she hadn't expected them.

"Alan, I can understand your being upset, but . . . I suppose they—the police—are just exploring all avenues, as Ted calls it. They think Lennie was at Shirley's last night."

"I see . . . and now they've got the idea *I'm* hiding him?"

"No, not that! But . . . he could be around, still. I suppose they think Lennie might try and get in touch."

Alan said, "He knows other people not far away—Friends of the hospital, for instance."

"Yes, they're checking on them, too."

Alan softened. None of this was Sally's direct concern. Lennie was *his* half brother, not hers. And Detective Sergeant Ted Hendricks should have had more sense than to use her as some sort of telephone exchange. "Thanks for letting me know, Sally. Let me do the worrying."

"I think the best thing for you to do, Alan, is to go around to the police station."

"No."

"What, then?"

"I don't know." He thought for a moment, his own breath amplified in his headpiece. "I think I'll take a run over to the hospital. Find out what happened. He escaped, you said?"

"Yes. From the laundry room or something."

"Look, Sally. Do me a favor. Ted is your big brother. Detective Sergeant Hendricks is somebody else. If he contacts you again, don't tell him where I've gone."

"All right, but . . ."

"What time will you be at home?"

"The usual, I hope."

"I'll come back to your place."

"I wish you would, Alan."

"Sorry if I lost my temper, Sally." He added, as if any silly bit of tenderness would somehow drive back this sudden horror, "You're pretty, you know?"

8

"Oh, Alan! I'm sorry . . . sorry."

Alan let himself out quietly through the front door and collected his Suzuki, half surprised that Hendricks wasn't waiting for him outside. The streets were fresh with a new April shower. Passers-by folded their umbrellas and avoided the puddles. The clouds were streaking away across the roof-tops, leaving an ocean of dark blue sky behind.

With no thought for anything else, Alan shot past the traffic, sometimes drifting across the white central lines.

So Lennie was out. Why had he done that—just frustration? He'd been in institutions for years.

More than once in the past Lennie had gone adrift, on his way to visit somebody or on the journey back to the hospital. Occasionally he'd be gone for days on end . . . so recently the hospital had clamped down. They'd tried to ensure that he was supervised on his little weekend jaunts. To Friends, as they were called—people who visited the hospital and offered open house. Nice, respectable people—even half brother Gordon down in Norbury. Lennie never stayed with Shirley, of course. Nor did he come often to visit Alan, either—Alan hadn't a house of his own with flower beds to be trampled down and glassware to be smashed in a tantrum or pets to be gouged at with sticks.

No, it took a good solid citizen to provide all those amenities for Lennie.

But Alan had collected him sometimes from the hospital. They trusted him as a companion for Lennie. Football. Cricket. A trip to the movies—so long as he returned Lennie safe in the evenings, safe and clean and not too mad.

But Lennie had made his own rules this time. Got out, taken off . . . Why to Shirley's, though? And why throttle Maggie Jones in passing?

And where was he now, at this moment? Walking a pavement? Lurking in an alley? In search of Alan, as Sally's big

9

brother seemed to think? Hate in his burnished eyes, just as it always was, the inexplicable, long hate—but no. Lennie wasn't very bright, only cunning. If he'd stuck around the scene of the crime since last night, surely he'd have been picked up by now.

All the same, in Brixton near the hospital the sweat came back, that ridiculous, irrational sense of foreboding which haunted Alan whenever Lennie was on the loose, with or without someone's leave.

He brushed a glove across his riding goggles as a new shower began and for an instant had a distorted image of Lennie . . . Lennie lying in wait. Then Alan was swinging his machine through the hospital gates on the hill. He fought down an impulse to go back—back at once. Suppose Lennie was still not far from the common, some desperate idea in his crazy head? Suppose he called on Sally! Absurd?

Just once they'd both taken him out to tea. And Sally had been nice to Lennie—that was a mistake! The mouth had grinned, the eyes had glowed with a false vacancy across the little white-covered table as Sally smiled and tried to start a conversation. She'd been good with Lennie—and Lennie never forgot a kindness.

That was the trouble, thought Alan, kicking his bike onto its stand and starting up the steps: Lennie never forgot a kindness!

Alan decided to make this quick.

chapter 2

The hospital was big and square and Victorian, as inspiring as a crematorium despite its reputation for modern and enlightened methods of treatment. Even the central heating system was primitive with thin, white smoke oozing out of tall Gothic chimneys to drift across a neighboring estate.

Alan didn't know whom he would get to see. The person in charge on Lennie's ward at least, he hoped; better still, perhaps a junior registrar.

So he was surprised when the blonde receptionist smiled at him through the window, asked him to wait, then picked up a phone. Afterward she said, "Doctor Zutmeyer will see you. Do you remember where his office is?"

"Yes, thanks."

It was as if Lennie's chief psychiatrist had expected him to call and left instructions at the desk.

Alan entered a tall, shabby room furnished in green, with plain green walls rising to chipped cornicing. An examination closet in one corner had a plastic curtain on rings with a three-foot tear in it as if some frenzied patient had once attacked it with a misplaced razor.

Doctor Zutmeyer waited at the desk, fingers entwined. "Ah, Mr. Bishop. We tried to contact you this morning, we thought without success."

"I just came along."

"I see." Emaciated features dwelled on Alan: a bony face, bony hands, an ivory-colored horn of a nose. It might have been only last week that Doctor Zutmeyer had crawled out of a Nazi gas chamber. "We wanted you to know the facts at first hand."

"All I know for sure is that Lennie escaped."

"*Escaped,* Mr. Bishop? But he is in care with us, not undergoing a life sentence of penal servitude! However, it is true that he . . . eluded surveillance. He took everyone by surprise."

"Why contact me—in particular?"

Doctor Zutmeyer shrugged. "You were the closest."

"You mean—nearest? Our half brother, Gordon, lives in Norbury."

A small curl of the thin lips. "Perhaps I meant . . . closest to Lennie. In age, interests. And less, shall we say, encumbered?"

Alan said, more sharply than he'd intended, "Interests! It's a pity he killed someone on the way out."

"Hardly on the way *out,* Mr. Bishop. And I gather that, so far, the police have only circumstantial evidence."

"They seemed to think he was at . . . our half sister's last night. Shirley. She and Maggie Jones shared a flat. It's close to the common."

"Ah, yes, Shirley. Lennie has mentioned her. Mr. Bishop, can you think of any reason why he should go there?" A slightly prurient gesture. "Surely not for the purposes of . . ."

"No! Shirley just might have been a soft touch."

"I beg your pardon?"

"She's free and easy with her money. She may have given him some."

"I'm not sure that Lennie would be motivated in that way.

12

If he was given money, however, that would enable him to travel farther afield, wouldn't it? Visit a different member of your family, perhaps.''

''Family?''

A light, somehow ironic rise of eyebrows, then an apparent change of subject. ''Between these four walls, Mr. Bishop, I do feel the police are rather jumping the gun, wouldn't you agree?''

Alan shook his head vaguely, wishing he could feel more at ease. Doctor Zutmeyer's gaze held all the charm of a decomposing corpse! ''My guess is that they'll run him to earth soon enough. There's a big hunt going on this time. I doubt, though, whether even if the police did try questioning him they'd get much sense out of Lennie. Do you?''

The enigmatic smile again, ''No, Mr. Bishop—but *I* might! Of course, we may have every confidence in the law's impartiality. Nevertheless, let us trust that when Lennie is found he'll be sent straight back here, as we've requested, and not be subjected to police interrogation. Frightened, disorientated, in what he will regard as hostile surroundings, he may even be capable of confessing to a crime he didn't commit. That would be most unfortunate.''

Doctor Zutmeyer arched his fingers. ''Not, of course, that if Lennie were arrested he'd be found fit to plead. But that is scarcely the point. The stigma . . . many months of careful treatment virtually wasted. Authorities are, alas, often intransigent in cases such as this.''

The doctor again turned his gaze on Alan. ''Naturally, if Lennie did kill that young woman then I'm afraid our hands will be tied. If not, and yet suspicion continues to be attached to him, the best we can expect is for pressures to be brought to bear upon us here at the hospital. At worst, Lennie will be transferred to an alternative institution where, if I may so put it, the regime will be . . . less flexible. In either case, the possibility of his future rehabilitation will be sacrificed. Do you follow my drift, Mr. Bishop?''

Alan wasn't sure. The psychiatrist's face, leaning forward slightly, was even more unfathomable than his slightly guttural and stilted prose. Shades of Himmler, perhaps—or some obscure attempt to involve Alan in hospital politics? Alan suddenly preferred the crude ironies of the brash young lawyer dissecting the unfortunate Mr. Gimble that morning.

For the first time he noticed a row of cassettes on a shelf above the bookcase, each labeled—with a name? Yes. He recalled from an earlier visit seeing a cassette recorder on the desk, partially hidden behind a pile of books. A patient had been on his way out—after an interview, recorded on the machine, later to be transcribed for his confidential file?

At first it seemed of only technical interest, part of an idle glance round the office to avoid Doctor Zutmeyer's haunting stare.

He switched his attention back, having missed part of what the psychiatrist was saying. ''It may be, Mr. Bishop, that Lennie will come to you—possibly with no idea of the events in which he is alleged to be implicated. Alternatively, you may know better than us—or the police—where to look for him. If, that is, he stays out of their clutches much longer.''

Alan forced a grin. ''You've got it all wrong, Doctor. Why should I know where he's gone?''

''A passing thought, Mr. Bishop. No more.''

Alan was baffled. He shrugged hopelessly and said, surprising himself with the words which sprang unwittingly to his lips, ''Suppose I choke him with my bare hands—before I bring him back?''

The eyes dropped immediately, perhaps in alarm, to Alan's side of the desk. ''Your bare *hands*, Mr. Bishop? Surely you would do no such thing—to a brother?''

14

Wouldn't—thought Alan. Or *couldn't?*

The phone rang, Doctor Zutmeyer picked up the receiver, listened for a moment, then replaced it. "Please excuse me, Mr. Bishop. An emergency. We'll be in touch again, perhaps? If there is news at this end, we have your office number."

He vanished through the door, leaving Alan to follow.

It had all taken up too much time—perhaps vital time, Alan thought. The late afternoon sky was gusty with rain spattering on his tinted goggles. In Brixton there was a snarl-up of traffic, with approaching drivers giving their own interpretation of the highway code: either plunging at him out of the dim, wet gloom like blind bats or using their headlights as wrecking rays.

There had been three cassettes, but he'd helped himself to only one, as if that would divide his guilt by three.

Damn silly thing to do! The tape probably wouldn't make jolly listening, Lennie uttering nothings through his thick, twisted lips, complaining that his cereal was cold at breakfast or pouring out the usual incoherent fantasies which beckoned you into the shadows of his madness.

Pocketing the thing had been little more than an irrational impulse—or so Alan told himself. Thus, in a time of crisis, the subconscious mind makes its own decisions, searches out its own path through a jungle of things half remembered, half forgotten . . .

His nerves still jangling, Alan rode much too fast back to Clapham—as if reckless speed alone were a substitute for real action, a short cut to decision. And Doctor Zutmeyer's cryptic, apparently senseless remark repeated itself over and over in his mind: "You may know better than us—or the police—where to look for Lennie . . ."

So okay, Doc—I'm looking!

He rode much more slowly through Tooting Bec, and made a slow patrol of the back streets near his room. No Lennie, of course. No crawling of the skin, either!

He wanted to hear the latest radio bulletin but could do without another encounter with Mrs. Friday, so he headed for the office and got there just as another heavy shower hit the elm trees around the scrubby little parking lot.

"Hi, Bish. Chiefy's asking after you. Thinks you've turned foreign correspondent."

"Know what he wants?"

"Overtime, what else? Oh, well, the money will be useful. Heard the latest about Maggie Jones?"

"No."

"They're looking for a psycho. If you're taking any short cuts across the common, Bish, you'd better go with a friend!"

Alan thought of asking how long ago the other reporter had picked up this information but didn't want to show too much interest.

He went through to the news editor's office and collected his evening's assignments: a local political meeting, and the mayor was visiting an old folks' home not far out of Clapham.

It occurred to Alan that the jobs would keep him out of the way for a bit—away from Sergeant Hendricks in particular. Lennie *could* turn up at any moment. They probably still had dogs sniffing along the footpaths on the common. Alan hoped *they'd* go in pairs, too!

Sally would be home by now. Alan felt a moment's new apprehension as he opened his overworked throttle and headed back across a different stretch of the common. The trees had a shroud of mist, and the sun was a swollen red balloon flickering in his goggles through overhead branches.

Sally was rinsing left-over dishes in her little kitchen. She

16

could only just afford the luxury of the tiny self-contained apartment to which Alan had a key. She looked up and smiled, dark hair wispy over her eyes. "Hungry?"

"If I stop to think about it."

"Go and turn the fire on. Have you finished for the day?"

"No. Got a couple of jobs."

"Where?"

"Just around town."

"Cup of tea to get on with?"

Alan went into the living room, stripped off his damp riding suit, placed his helmet carefully upside down on the table. When Sally came in he was tugging the cassette out of his pocket.

"What have you got there?"

"T.S. Eliot. *The Waste Land.*"

"Really?"

"No!"

Her eyes brooded over teacups. "I don't really know what to say, Alan."

"That's okay, honey."

"These jobs you mentioned—will they take long?"

"Not if I can do a bit of guesswork and skimp them a bit. You want to go somewhere?"

"No. It's Ted again."

"What about him?"

"He's still using me as a telephone. He wants to see you—unofficially, he said."

"Where and when?"

"About six, at the Dark Angel, at the bar."

"That sounds hospitable—and rather definite."

"Can you make it?"

"What happens if I don't? Do they send out an all-points bulletin for me?"

"You know it isn't like that."

17

"I hope! Any of yesterday's meat pie left?"

"Yes. Bread and butter?"

"Thanks." She left the tea steaming and went back to the kitchen.

"How was the inspection?"

"Ghastly. Little Gwen upset a jar of red paint all down one of their skirts."

"Good for little Gwen!"

Sally returned with the food on a tray. She said, "That cassette. It's got Lennie's name on it."

"Clever girl!"

"They gave it to you at the hospital?"

"Not exactly!"

Then, "It's a record of an interview with his psychiatrist?"

"I can see why they're making you Teacher of the Year— or would, but for little Gwen."

"Do you mind if I say something else?"

"Shoot."

"About Lennie. Alan, I know you feel . . . responsible. He was always closest to you, wasn't he?"

"You too? That's what his psychiatrist seems to think. Yes, Lennie's close—like a hair shirt!"

"I put it badly. Sorry. But Alan, you've been dodging Ted all day. Why?"

"Perhaps because he always makes me feel like a kid of ten."

"Now you're trying to dodge *me!* Alan, I'm only guessing, but you'd like to find Lennie yourself, wouldn't you? Before the police catch up with him."

"That's news to me. Anyway, I haven't done very well so far. There hasn't been much time, has there?"

"Does that mean yes?"

18

"Suppose I tell you I just don't know? How I feel, that is, and what I think. I'm leaving all that to you and Doctor Zutmeyer! What did you do—have lunch with him?"

"I'm sorry. I'm interfering—it isn't really my business. Except . . ."

"Go on."

"I know how you've suffered because of Lennie. You, far more than anybody else in your . . . family. From things you've told me, things I've seen."

"You don't know the half of it," said Alan, wishing he'd bitten the words back.

Sally waited, looking into his face, before she went on. "I don't want to—not if you'd rather not tell me. And it's not Lennie I care about—it's you. Alan, whatever that psychiatrist said, don't get involved—not any more than you have to. And if you don't want to talk to Ted, there are other policemen."

Alan grinned. "Who am I to turn down a free half pint at the pub?" He glanced at his watch. "I'll be back as soon as possible. And Sally . . ." He wondered how to put it without sounding ridiculously melodramatic, "If anybody knocks on the door, don't answer. Right?"

Sally frowned. "You don't think Lennie would come here?"

"Not really."

"We never brought him back to the apartment."

"I may have mentioned the address."

"Lennie wouldn't remember a thing like that."

"You're joking. Lennie has a very good sense of direction, but skip it."

"He's probably miles away by now."

"Doing what?"

"Just running away. Running—for the sake of it."

Alan began putting his riding suit on. "Tell you something, honey baby? Brother Lennie never does anything just for the sake of it."

"You've eaten hardly anything."

"If you make that meat pie into a sandwich, I'll take it with me."

She went into the kitchen again and returned with a paper bag. "It's hardly half past five. Why the rush?"

When Alan didn't answer she popped the bag into his up-turned helmet. "I may be asleep when you come in. You've got the key? Softly, softly, mind, or you'll ruin my reputation."

Alan kissed her on the nose. "I thought little Gwen had already done that!"

chapter 3

He'd wanted a little time before meeting Hendricks—time, wasted or not, to cruise in and out of the glistening streets, searching every shadowed corner, every darkening alley entrance and shop doorway. He found nothing, of course. But once he passed a lurking patrol car with its lights extinguished. Evidently the police hadn't had any better luck.

Alan parked behind the Dark Angel a few minutes after six. Hendricks was waiting. For such a young man he had an air of dissolute flabbiness: prematurely balding head, glassy eyes swimming in a curiously characterless face, carelessly worn clothes covering his big frame. A plain, badly knotted tie revealed a shirt button.

Hendricks watched Alan come through the swinging door, showing no apparent interest. The bar, practically deserted, was fitted with benched alcoves. Alan slid into a seat, and Hendricks gave him a casual nod before unpeeling a small cigar and lighting it, squinting his eyes enigmatically through the smoke.

He took his time about going to the bar and coming back with two halves of bitter, which he plonked down on the table. "Cheers."

"Cheers. Cozy little place, this. Do you come here often?"

"Not often."

Alan was never sure of his ground with Hendricks. He

resorted to the usual defensive banter for which he always afterward despised himself. "This is where you bring your suspects? What do you do when they don't confess—bang their heads on the partition?"

Hendricks grinned, big mouth showing two broken teeth. "Who would you have in mind, exactly?"

"Sally said you wanted to see me."

"Yes. Thanks for taking the trouble."

"She said it was unofficial."

"That's right."

"If you think I can help you find Lennie . . ."

"It was just a thought."

"Do I call you Ted or Sergeant?"

The eyes narrowed again through fresh smoke. "We can do better than this, don't you think?"

"Sorry. What have I done wrong?"

"You're very strung up, Alan."

"What do you expect? You haven't found Lennie yet, have you?"

"Worried?"

"Of course! Aren't your people?"

"You could say that. We've had men out all day on the common—and dogs. All they've come up with so far are toadstools."

Alan wished, as always, that he hadn't behaved like an inept teenager with Sally's brother. He began doing his thing with his pipe. Clenching it between his teeth, he dragged the pouch out of his right-hand pocket and passed it to the left, where he could clamp it while he stuffed tobacco in. Then, twisting the stem at forty-five degrees in his mouth, he one-handedly struck a match and sucked in the flame, finally tonguing the pipe back to a smokable angle.

Hendricks watched bemusedly. "I suppose you're lucky it's your left hand."

22

Alan shrugged. "I'm left-handed."

"I didn't know."

"I never told you. Look, what can I do for you—Sergeant? I've got some evening assignments."

"So have I, old lad," said Hendricks. "The small talk was your idea, not mine. I'll fill you in with the background. You know how things work, Alan? Every morning after reveille we sergeants are put on parade and dished out our good deeds for the day. I drew the short straw on this one. It may not be entirely chance. You couldn't expect him to admit it, but my superintendent probably found out that I knew you personally. Normally, of course, that sort of thing is *infra dig* but in this case . . ."

"Why in this case?"

"We all want Lennie back and fast, for his own sake, perhaps. To be candid, the case against him is far from cut and dried. We need Lennie himself to establish it one way or the other."

"If you're expecting Lennie to give intelligent answers to your questions . . ."

"He won't have to, Alan. Forensic will do that for him. Clothing, fingernails, the usual stuff. Only the sooner the better. If Lennie didn't do it then someone else did, and he's getting a headstart on us. Those are the obvious reasons for the hurry."

"And the less obvious?"

"Shall we call them political—or do I mean sociological? My super's a sensitive guy. He lies awake at night worrying about the heat that's always generated when a psycho gets loose and runs amok. This case could snowball, Alan, and become something of a national outcry. That also gives my super ulcers—the way the media can make the police look like a lot of balloons bumping into each other. Task forces. Crime squads. Murder controls. Too many police administrators, they say, trying to keep up with what goes on on television."

Alan removed his pipe from his mouth, laid it beside him on the bench, took a swig at his tankard, then put the pipe back before it went out. "What actual evidence is there that Lennie did kill Maggie Jones?"

"We have a witness who picked out Lennie's mug shot down at the station. However, she admits to having been a long way off at the time. She's a bit of an insomniac, apparently, and often takes a stroll along the edge of the common as late as midnight. I fancy she won't be doing it again for a little while! Anyway, she saw a figure belting through the bushes. Personally, between you and me, either it was a sheer fluke, her picking that photo out, or she's psychic. The moon was out, but to be that sure she'd have needed Halley's Comet to see by. It could tie in, though. You see, I'm pretty certain Lennie was at your sister's last night—within a stone's throw."

"My *half* sister's."

"All right, your half sister's."

"You said *pretty* sure."

Hendricks showed his broken teeth again. "For some reason, your Shirley wasn't in a hurry to admit it."

"You interviewed her?"

"Of course."

"But if Shirley denied seeing Lennie . . ."

"We found a sweater hanging on a chair in the bathroom. Plain gray, hospital laundry markings. He'll be feeling cold without it."

"He could have left it there on some other occasion."

"You think so?"

"You've been to the hospital, too!"

"We haven't spent the day down at the station playing dominoes, old lad!"

24

"And that's where you got his photo—the mug shot you mentioned?"

The smoky gaze again. "Where else? Lennie hasn't got a criminal record has he?"

Alan gulped at his beer. "Surely you'd know if he had, Sergeant?"

"Possibly."

"If you want my opinion, it all doesn't make sense. If Lennie was at Shirley's, why wait until Maggie had gone out, then go after her on the common? And look—if Maggie was molested . . ."

"She wasn't," said Hendricks. "And we do know about Lennie's sexual immaturity."

"Then why should he strangle her?"

"Money. Maggie's handbag was found near the body. Cleaned out."

"That doesn't prove she had any with her at the time."

"Who, Maggie?"

"That's something else you may have wrong, Sergeant. Maggie and Shirley are what you call class. They don't go out soliciting on moonlit nights under a spreading chestnut tree."

"No," said Hendricks. "We won't call you, you call us!' I do know the facts of life, old lad. As a matter of fact, Maggie was taking her pekinese for a wee—it ran home afterward. Maybe poor Maggie was an insomniac, too. By the way, Alan, you said Lennie wouldn't give us intelligent answers. How bright is he?"

"It depends what you mean by intelligence."

"Oh, come on, you can do better than that."

"That expert would be Lennie's psychiatrist. Ask him nicely, and he might even give you his I.Q. Or have you interviewed *him* already?"

Hendricks said cheerfully. "Ah, Doctor Zutmeyer by

name. Yes, we interviewed him—sort of. We should have worn good old-fashioned English police helmets—attitudes die hard, to coin a phrase. He treated us like the Gestapo. Mind you, nobody at the hospital was very cooperative. I'm afraid we may have to lean on them a little. There must be reports on Lennie, mustn't there?"

"So?"

"They'd give us a few clues, wouldn't they? About what makes Lennie tick, what was in his mind, how he'd behave in certain situations."

Alan concentrated on his pipe. "If you're going to read Lennie's dossier, you'd better brush up on your Chinese."

Hendricks said, blandly, "Now, this is where we get down to the nitty gritty, Alan. Anything you can tell us about Lennie will help. I gather he's turned up on your doorstep at times."

"I haven't got a doorstep."

"Just a bit younger than you, isn't he?"

"About a year."

The shrewd, half-mocking stare again: "Allowing for obvious differences—hair style and so on—you're alike, did you know?"

"Are we?"

"You took him out occasionally. Sally and I don't gossip about your private affairs, but she did mention a football game. By the way, can you manage another of those?" He pointed to the empty tankard.

"Thanks. It's my round."

"Forget it. It's all on the taxpayer."

While Hendricks was at the bar, Alan thought of the football game. Chelsea playing Southampton. On the way in he'd bought Lennie a scarf. Stupid thing to do!

After the final whistle there'd been a bit of jostling on the terrace. Nothing too serious; a bunch of kids up from Southampton on the bus were feeling a bit high because their team had beaten hell out of Chelsea.

They'd come dancing along the litter-strewn steps, flicking their scarves at anyone within reach. One of the kids caught Lennie in the face, and before Alan could do anything about it he'd unwound his new scarf and got the kid down on the bare stone in a strangle grip. By the time Alan had somehow freed Lennie's hand, the boy's tongue was practically hanging out.

Hendricks put the new tankards down. "It's beginning to occur to us, Alan, that Lennie may have found another doorstep. Of course we're checking, but you could save us a bit of trouble with a few addresses. Let me see, isn't there another half brother—*Gordon* Bishop?"

"Yes. He lives in Norbury. I'll jot his address down in your notebook if you like, Sergeant. He's older than me. Got a nice little wife, if you like her type. Winner of a local beauty contest—icy as the top of a wedding cake. When you get around to interviewing him, mind you don't trip over his mortgage!"

Alan hopefully glanced at his watch. Hendricks was unimpressed. "It's odd you all seem to have stuck to the name Bishop."

"You know about Lennie's dad? His name isn't Bishop. It's Henry Larkins. Lives under a boat on some beach in Essex, near Benfleet, I think. You can probably skip seeing him, Sergeant. Henry wouldn't give anybody an empty whisky bottle, let alone help Lennie."

"Drink problem?"

"No, solution! Next question?"

"Your mother . . ." Hendricks looked uncomfortable. "Believe it or not, I don't want to be personal."

"Oh, be as personal as you like, Sergeant. I'll tell you what you may know already. Our mother was in what less

27

permissive times used to be called the village tart. Now and then, something would go wrong—or right, depending on how you look at it. She fell for kids. Five, so far as I know. One's dead. Another's mad. One's in Mom's old profession, only she has more finesse. I'm the fourth." Alan vaguely flicked his withered hand. "Don't worry, Sergeant. When the time comes to ask your permission to marry Sally, I shall make a point of mentioning that our family background isn't all bad. There's always dear old Gordon. He's the bank clerk in Norbury."

Hendricks looked astonished. "What's eating you, old lad? If you want to marry my sister don't ask me. We were talking about your mother—Mrs. Bishop?"

Alan was appalled to find that his hand was shaking and tried to calm himself down. "Not any more. She didn't give her favors for nothing, you know. About a year back she bought some sort of guest house in Southend on Sea. A place called Fairview, I think, at the shabby end of the promenade. I haven't seen her since she made herself an honest woman. Married a bloke called Frank somebody. Haines. That's it. Frank Haines. How am I doing?

"Very well. This village where you were all brought up. Salt Lea, in Essex, wasn't it?"

"You seem to know."

"Any relatives still there?"

"Relatives?"

"I take it that means no."

"You can't imagine Lennie would . . . ?"

"Run off to Salt Lea—or Southend?" said Hendricks, getting up. "Who knows? Every possibility has to be checked, hasn't it?" A pause that may have meant nothing. "Just one more thing . . ."

"Yes?"

"I gather Lennie's gone adrift before—A.W.O.L. so to

speak. Three times, wasn't it? Ever find out where he went then, Alan?''

"I don't think anybody did. The general theory is that he just bummed around, slept in the open for a night or two, begged off strangers—I don't know."

"Lennie's capable of that?"

"Yes."

"And looking after himself—keeping clean, that sort of thing?"

"Up to a point. Why do you ask?"

"It struck us as a bit unexpected, that's all. We had a chat with a charge nurse over at the hospital this morning. On the last occasion Lennie was missing—for what, four days?—he came back under his own steam, and the nurse says he was quite spruce, considering. Fingernails trimmed, shirt freshly ironed—he'd even had a haircut! What do you make of it, Alan? Who did all that for Lennie—the Salvation Army? Or some kindly soul—a hospital Friend, as they call them, who never let on? You look puzzled yourself, Alan."

"Yes—if that nurse's memory isn't playing tricks."

"Well, we'll keep plugging away—and collecting addresses. If you get any ideas, you will let us know?"

"Yes . . . of course."

Hendricks recovered the notebook in which Alan had been scribbling. Then he nodded amiably at Alan's tankard. "I shouldn't finish that, old lad. You've just spilt pipe ash into it. You'll poison yourself with nicotine!"

The political meeting was as dull as most. Alan sat as close to the front as he could, propping his miniature tape recorder on his knee and switching it on in order to pick up the voice of the main speaker. The speech was mercifully short and wouldn't be too much trouble to condense later on. Then he left the machine running for about five minutes of question time, hoped he had enough material for a half column and slipped away.

At the old people's home a local magician of modest talent was manipulating colored balls attached to supposedly invisible elastic bands up his sleeve. Alan chatted with the mayor, collected a few homey remarks from a bright-eyed octogenarian and made a second discreet departure before they brought on the soprano.

It was after eight. Yet another shower splashed down in the street outside, and a single crackle of distant lightning split a now moonless sky.

A telephone booth glowed dimly on the opposite pavement. Alan made a couple of quick calls. Shirley gave him her careful Mayfair voice, but there were breaks in it as if she'd been crying. Gordon was predictably petulant and exaggeratedly discreet, as though the post office computer might have been programmed to pick up what he said, take it down and use it as evidence.

Alan emerged, wiped the saddle of his bike with his handkerchief and set off for Norbury. As long as he could evade the traffic police he reckoned he could make it in twenty minutes.

chapter 4

Gordon waited patiently while Alan peeled off his riding gear in the doorway. Then he fastidiously took it from him and hung it carefully on a peg. "I wonder you don't get yourself a nice little car."

They went into an impeccably furnished living room: color TV, thick wall-to-wall carpeting, a do-it-yourself decor borrowed from a Sunday supplement.

"Well, take a pew. Drink? I've got sherry, gin and beer."

"Beer—thanks."

Gordon opened the door of a highly polished mahogany-veneered cabinet. He poured Alan's beer into a sparkling glass and helped himself to a stiff gin and tonic. "Long time no see. You didn't even send a Christmas card."

"I don't remember getting one from you, either!"

Gordon had soft sandy hair, neatly styled and matching his modest moustache. Even at that hour he had a pink, well, shaven look, fawn lambs-wool pull-over, trousers well creased, leather slippers. "By the way, Angela sends her best. She's gone to bed. Not too fit at the moment."

"Sorry."

"You needn't be. As a matter of fact, we're expecting a baby in June."

"Congratulations."

"Yes . . ." Gordon dropped his eyes to his glass. "I'm keeping my fingers crossed that it won't have two heads or be schizophrenic or something."

"That's ridiculous!"

"Is it? Perhaps we all suffer from not having a photo of Grannie on the mantlepiece. Doesn't the irony ever run through *your* mind, Alan? 'What did Daddy do in the war, Mommy?' 'I don't know, dear. I only met him the once.' By the way, I have heard the news."

"I can guess how you feel."

"Can? For one thing I feel I should have had my name changed officially long ago. A bit late now, isn't it."

"Like the old joke about Charlie Stinks."

"Sorry?"

"He had his name changed to *Billie* Stinks."

Gordon got up and replenished his glass from the cabinet. "I suppose you've come down here about Lennie. Why? Don't tell me you're trying to cash in on an exclusive story for your rag?"

"You think I'm capable of that?"

"Apologies, sonny. You simply donned your suit of rubber armor and set out on your metal charger in search of Lennie. Why can't you just leave him to the police?"

"In a way I'm trying to help the police."

"Who, you?" Gordon's laugh was brittle. "That's a bit bizarre isn't it? Still, there always was something unbearably noble about you, Alan. Possibly, though, noble is the wrong word."

"Thanks!"

"Well, I take it you're satisfied that Lennie isn't here? Unless you want to search the attic. To be quite frank, the little monster's of no interest to me."

Alan shook his head. "I just wanted your ideas. After all, we both have a responsibility for Lennie."

Gordon's eyes glazed over as if he'd used a switch. "Oh, I see! Sorry, old boy. No dice. If you're interested in the remote past, you'd better join an archaeological society. Count me out. If it's of any help, we last saw Lennie about six months ago.''

"And?''

"We made a mistake, buying a house so close to the hospital. He has a habit, every now and again, of turning up here to scrounge.''

"So you threw him out?''

"Not at all. As a matter of fact, he stayed the night. Ate us out of house and home and vanished the next day without so much as a goodbye. Correction! It wasn't as simple as that— he lifted five pounds from a drawer upstairs.''

"What did you do about it?''

"Do?''

"The money.''

"What could I do? It was my own fault for not having the drawers fitted with padlocks. We all know Lennie's little ways, don't we?''

"He just turned up—on that occasion, I mean?''

"Not exactly. Somebody at the hospital phoned beforehand. 'Please can you look after our boa constrictor for the weekend? It's quite harmless, if you don't get too close'.''

"He made his own way back to the hospital?''

"Eventually. I gather it was several days before he wandered into his cage. The hospital seemed to think it was my fault—kept ringing up at all hours. More or less asked if I'd buried him at the bottom of the garden.''

"Did they get the police?''

"I don't know. I doubt it. Lennie was supposed to be harmless, wasn't he? Now they know better! Can I fill you up?''

"No thanks, I mustn't stay.''

Gordon's sigh of relief was barely audible. He poured himself a third gin, but instead of bringing it back to his chair he leaned against the cabinet and said, "Look here Alan, there are some things you'd better get straight. Between us, for instance. You think I despise you, but actually it's the other way around, isn't it? Why? Because, some time ago, I made up my mind what sort of life I was going to live. I'm a bank clerk and I earn four thousand a year. I haven't got much social conscience and even less imagination. I'd probably refuse an overdraft to the young Henry Ford! I'll tell you more, Alan, I vote Conservative and belong to the Taxpayers Association. I've got plastic gnomes on my lawn, and I wash my car every Sunday morning. Got it? My upbringing, if you can call it that, isn't going to ruin the rest of my life. To hell with Mrs. Bishop, and even more to hell with Lennie. You think I haven't had a bellyful of that little creep? Even when we were kids he'd pipe and we'd dance—as if you didn't know. So far as I'm concerned, I don't care if he killed that tart or not. The police can draw their guns and shoot him down on sight. Do I make myself clear?"

"Clear enough," said Alan, getting up. He replaced his glass on the cabinet top, hoping it wouldn't leave a stain. "You'd better watch that gin, Gordon. It goes to your head rather fast. And by the way, a brotherly warning. I'm afraid the police will probably give you a call. Don't worry, I'll use my influence and ask them to switch off the siren at the corner of the avenue."

The rain had cleared. Back in Clapham, half an hour later, Alan propped his Suzuki against a wall in the moonlight and walked up a short flight of steps.

There was a bell to push, one of several, and the door opened automatically at the behest of someone occupying the first floor apartment.

Shirley Bishop looked petite, dressed chastely in white with a string of ivory beads and large matching earrings. She was very dark-skinned, with the high cheekbones of a Masai, though some ancestor had probably made a long, enforced detour through the Caribbean.

She sounded cheerful enough, smiling at Alan and slipping back into the mid-Atlantic drawl she affected when she wasn't on the telephone. "Get out of that gear boy, and take the weight off your feet."

"Everybody's offering me seats tonight."

"Maybe they don't like the way you wear out their carpets."

There was a couch embroidered with silver lace, and ample scatter pillows. Alan squatted on the edge of a chair, and Shirley curled herself languidly on the couch. A little white pekinese came huffing and puffing from somewhere and jumped up beside her. She stroked it, her eyelids drooping.

"Shirley, I'm sorry."

"That's okay. She was a nice kid. All day long I've been seeing her face, you know? Then suddenly it was gone. Even her face was gone, like she'd never been. Help yourself to a drink, if you want."

"No thanks."

"You said you wanted to talk about Lennie. You working with the police?"

"Who, me? You have to be five-foot-ten or something. That counts me out."

"That little contraption you carry about in your jacket . . ."

Alan fished out his Grundig and tossed it on the couch beside her. "Look, you don't have to treat me like a secret agent. Play it back, if you like. You'll hear Councilor Hopkins leading on about the local drainage system and an appropriate gurgle from an old lady who was eighty-five on her last birthday.''

Shirley ignored the machine. ''You know the trouble with our family, Alan? We don't trust each other. Never did.''

''We can always try. Alan smiled. ''For instance, tell me—Lennie *was* here last night, wasn't he?''

''What's it to you? Don't tell me you're still hung up on saving his goddamn soul! The answer's yes, okay, he did pop by—sort of.''

''What time was that?''

''Pretty late, I guess.''

''Why deny it to the police?''

''The police!'' Her teeth shone. ''Force of habit, boy. Maggie and me always made a point of giving them a wide berth.''

''But if they find out for sure that you lied . . .''

''How are they going to do that unless you tell them?''

''He left his sweater in the bathroom.''

''Oh, yeah, I found it, after I'd thrown him out. I don't know why the crazy kid took it off—maybe he reckoned on staying the night. I didn't notice he was wearing it in the first place. I even gave him a zip-up jacket that was lying around.''

''The police should have been told about that, you know. It alters his description a bit. Anyway, what did Lennie want? Not just a shoulder to cry on.''

''Are you kidding? Man, that kid needed comfort like I need a blood transfusion. He bounced me for five. He'd have made it ten, only I felt cheap.''

''You lent him five pounds?''

''Lent! Anyway, I gave him his handout and told him to skidaddle back to the hospital.''

36

"You thought he'd do that—on your say-so?"

"I didn't really care one way or the other. I just wanted him out of my hair. I never did like him hanging around here. Jeeze, those eyes!"

"If you'd told the police all this, they might have been less inclined to pin the murder on Lennie. They haven't got much of a case as it is."

"Okay, but so what? And quit preaching at me! Nothing's going to bring Maggie back. If Lennie choked her to death, he ought to be crucified, but I'm not helping the fuzz. Open your mouth, and before you know it you're standing in some goddamn courtroom being grilled. Bad for business, boy!"

"Look, Shirley, if you gave Lennie a fiver why would he take the trouble to go after Maggie, strangle her and clean out her handbag? Did you tell him she was out on the common?"

"No . . . but he could have seen her. I told you, I sold him a bit short."

"But with his brains Lennie would think five pounds was enough to get him all the way to New York."

"He isn't that thick, Alan. And sometimes Maggie asked for trouble. She was dumb in some ways. She even tried to be nice to Lennie whenever he turned up here. Where did that ever get anybody? And maybe he's grown into a man at last."

"But Maggie wasn't . . . molested. Her . . . clothing wasn't even disturbed."

"So your sergeant friend said. Crazy isn't it? Anyway, girls like us aren't easy to molest, as you so quaintly put it." She pensively stroked the pekinese.

"That's one of the reasons why Lennie's on the spot. Motive. The police know he's not exactly Casanova. That isn't the point, though, really."

"So when do we get to it?"

"Every now and then, he takes off for a few days. Nobody seems to know where. Sometimes, if not always, he grabs some cash for the trip. Last time it came from Gordon."

Shirley laughed. "I bet that hurt!"

Alan said, "Where does he go, I wonder?"

"Does it have to be anywhere in particular?"

"I think so."

"What gives you that idea?"

"Just a hunch."

"Yeah? Well, you know Lennie. He may be a moron, but he could find just about anybody without the help of a map. Somebody to pester, another handout, a free meal . . ."

"And somebody who'd cut his nails and iron his shirt?"

Shirley gasped. "Oh, dear Christ!"

"What does that mean?"

"Nothing—forget it."

"Oh, come on!"

"But it's crazy!"

"What is, for God's sake?"

She put the pekinese down and let it snuffle off. "I said, forget it, boy. I want to think. Correction. I *don't* want to think. Period!"

"You know where Lennie goes—perhaps where he is right now!"

"I didn't say that."

"Shirley, I want to know what's on your mind."

"What are you going to do—choke it out of me with your one good hand?"

Suddenly the bell rang in the corner, the bell connected to the front door. Alan asked, "You expecting a visitor?"

Shirley shook her hand. "No. Not tonight."

"Aren't you going to answer it?"

"To hell with it!"

"It could be the police again."

38

She smiled wickedly. "You think I'd corrupt the police?"

"Lennie?"

"Tell you something, Alan? That kid's getting under your skin, as usual. If it was Lennie, you think the police wouldn't have picked him up on the way through the gate? There's been a squad car out there most of the day."

Alan relaxed a bit. "It's probably some guy taking a chance that I'll open the door," Shirley said. "Maggie and I mostly send them packing. *Did* that is."

The bell didn't ring more than twice. Alan said, "Shirley . . ."

"Look, I told you, I'm not getting involved. Nothing's going to change that. If you want to know Lennie's little secret, if he has one, ask someone else. Why pick on me? I'm not the only member of this so-called family."

She switched expression, and subject, and Alan could only listen. "I've been thinking maybe I should change my life. Does that make you laugh? Take up yoga or learn to ski or find myself a respectable job in a London Transport canteen. Sometimes I feel trapped—right? Trapped behind glass, wondering how the hell to reach the world outside. Self-pity, I guess."

"It won't last, Shirley."

Alan gave up, for the moment. He pulled on his riding gear. "I'll be back."

"Yeah, sure. Anytime."

When he got downstairs, Alan hesitated on the steps. He listened for a moment to the wind in the trees, but there was none there. His bike leaned untouched against the wall.

chapter 5

It was still only Thursday—nearly midnight. Twenty-four hours ago at about this hour, Maggie Jones was still breathing, taking time off to walk her little pekinese on the common. Lennie had already left Shirley's, stuffing her five pounds into a pocket of the zip-up jacket she'd found for him.

There was a light on in Sally's flat. From her bedroom came the strains of smooth night music. Had she been awake and heard Alan coming, she would have called out.

Alan decided not to disturb her. The radio wouldn't wear out its batteries—it was fitted with a tiny device that automatically turned it off within an hour.

He moved stealthily into the kitchen and sneaked a cold sausage from the fridge—he'd eaten Sally's sandwich hours ago. He poured himself half a glass of milk and went back into the tiny living room, collecting Sally's cassette player on the way. He still had the tape in his pocket.

It ran ninety minutes—forty-five on each side. One of Doctor Zutmeyer's staff had printed Lennie's name on the front, then a recent date, but no other details.

Alan sprawled on the couch with the apparatus on his stomach. He slid in the cassette, turning the volume very low.

He came in in the middle of a sequence, apparently; Lennie's voice was a flat monotone, almost as if he'd been under hypnosis. There was no preliminary comment—the recording took up, presumably, from where a previous tape had ended.

". . . shut up with all these nutcases. Nutcases, that's all they are. Take my ward—around thirty of us in beds a couple of feet apart, and all these nuts going off bang like fireworks. They lay there all quiet, half dead with dope, then someone starts shouting his head off—for nothing. Yesterday it was because some guy said another guy had stolen his watch. That was crazy—the poor jerk never had a watch in the first place. Anyway, before you knew it, they was leaning over and trying to choke each other. Just a couple of old nuts. One of them would have got killed, I reckon, if the nurses hadn't come in. Swooped on them like vultures they did . . ."

There was evidently a lot more of this sort of thing. Alan pressed the fast forward button.

". . . the other night? There's this old geezer who sleeps next to me. They call him Freddie. Christ, he must be eighty odd, got a face like a lizard. He likes me, does Freddie. We talk a lot, crack jokes and that, and sometimes we play dominoes. Well, there he is with his eyes on me. Then he goes for me, puts his fingers around my throat and breathes on my face. Why did he do that? I done nothing to him. Well, I'm just blacking out when a couple of nurses come in, make a dive at poor old Freddie, stretch him on the bed like a scarecrow. Crazy old coot tries kicking them. That's nuts—I mean, you don't kick nurses, not if you don't want to get a going over, do you? Well, one of them sits on Freddie's feet while the other shoves the needle in. He lies there crying—crying like a baby for his mom. 'Mommy, Mommy, Mommy,'' he says. This morning he don't even remember what happened.''

Alan pushed the forward button again—and again. Still Lennie was droning on: "I got this temper, see? Gets me into trouble, at times. I see red and hit out. I start swearing and shouting things. Sometimes it takes half a dozen nurses to pin me down. When I'm really bad, they drag me off to this room. It's not a padded cell, like. Only it's all dark and bare and you know what?''

Doctor Zutmeyer's quiet voice, ''What, Lennie?''

''It's got a kinky mirror in it! Old Freddie told me. When you look into it, if there's enough light, you see your own face. But on the other side the nurses are looking in like it was a window.''

Lennie sniggered. ''They don't know that I know. It's easy to kid them nurses—they're not very bright, are they? Who'd do that sort of job if they was bright? Well, I got it worked out, if you go on kicking and screaming they'll watch you and leave you to starve if necessary. So I just sit all quiet by the wall and it isn't long before they let me out . . .''

And then, after one more push at the forward button, something different: ''. . . better again. When I'm better, they'll let me out, won't they? I mean—for keeps. I'll go back and live with my mom. She don't mind what I do. She just wants me to be happy, see? I'll go and live in my cave again. I often used to go and live in my cave. Once, when I was only a kid, I ran away and stayed there for near a week. I took cans of fruit and food. Nobody never found me. Only it got cold one night so I went back to my mom.''

''Was she angry with you Lennie?''

''Who, my mom? No!'' Lennie giggled. ''She's a bit soft, is my mom. I told you, she lets me do anything I like, except when my dad's around.''

Who, Mrs. Bishop? thought Alan. Soft? That was a laugh. Even Lennie should have remembered better than that.

''Your dad's stricter with you, Lennie?''

''Well, yeah. He used to be. Beat me up and that.'' A sudden plaintive note like that of a very small boy. ''Everybody beat me up. When I was living with my brothers—they was real bullies. Pushing me around and getting me into trouble. I used to run away to my cave. I had a mattress down there and blankets and that . . ."

The reel came to an abrupt end, and the machine clicked itself off. Alan stared at it, suddenly too tired to bother to reverse the cassette. What would it tell him that was new? Lennie's cave had been in a disused quarry near their old cottage in Salt Lea. Ted Hendricks had probably heard something about it from somebody. Sergeant-leave-no-stone-unturned Hendricks. Well, if so, he was years out of date.

Unless . . . well, it was possible. Lennie with his mixture of bird brain and cunning, homing in on a familiar funk hole where he'd think he was king of the castle? This time? The *other* times?

There was something wrong with that, though. Who'd cut his fingernails and spruced him up for the return journey? Henry Larkins? Mrs. Bishop down in Southend? *His mom and dad?*

No, something was wrong. And then there had been Shirley's sudden inspiration, followed by a clam-up. *"It's crazy . . . if you want to know Lennie's little secret, if he has one, ask someone else . . ."*

"Who, for instance?"

Alan pressed the eject button, turned the cassette over and tried to restart the machine. No go. The mechanism was stuck fast, or the damned motor had blown.

He was still fiddling with it when Sally appeared in the doorway. "You should have let me know you were back."

"I just thought that in the morning you'd have thirty six-year-olds crawling all over you. And the inspectors'll be hanging around waiting for you to fall into a carefully prepared trap."

"The midnight news woke me."

"News!"

"Somebody else has been shot in Ireland. A water main burst in Pimlico." She looked at the cassette recorder. "Anything interesting?"

"I've only heard the first half. It's gone phut."

"Again? I've been meaning to have it fixed."

"Never mind. I've got another back at my room."

"Will it keep till the morning?"

Alan grinned, despite everything. "Yes, it'll keep!

Alan was late at the office next day and busy all morning. Eventually he was sent to the scene of a fire.

The man who lived there was still shaking uncontrollably. It turned out that he'd refused to go in the ambulance and declined to accept any sedation from the medical staff on the spot.

He was big and hefty and belligerent. His eyes were bloodshot from the smoke, and the dark stubble on his chin resembled a black fungus sprouting from a pasty mask of face.

Alan talked to him on his doorstep, recorder switched on. The stench of burned furniture—and worse—still drifted down a scorched stairway. The man kept the door half-closed and said, "If you must know, the name's Billings."

"Thanks." Alan nodded.

"Didn't take you vultures long to get here, did it? Couple of seconds earlier and I'd have had the kids out. Couldn't make it. Flames beat me back halfway up the stairs. Filthy fire brigade was late, finishing their card game I suppose."

"Names of the children?" asked Alan gently.

"Patsy, Rebecca. They'd have been at school, only they was just getting over measles. You ain't interviewing the wife."

"I understand."

"You *what?* Listen, sonny. You don't understand anything! All you care about is stuffing your rag with other people's tragedies. *Clapham and Tooting Weekly?* I buy it, now and again, to stand my muddy boots on. Look, if you want to do something useful, try hammering the Council. Bloody rat traps, these places. All matchwood and plaster. Good enough for the workers, of course. Makes me laugh.''

But at that moment it seemed improbable that Mr. Billings would ever laugh again.

Hendricks intercepted Alan fifty yards along the street. His round, pudding face managed to look sympathetic. ''They told me you'd probably be here. You look as though you could use a drink.''

All Alan could think of to say was, ''If they ever bring in prohibition, Sergeant, you'll be done for.''

They went to a different bar. ''That fire was a nasty mess,'' said Hendricks.

Alan said, ''Poor bastard! He's been unemployed for weeks. Wife's got a steady job at Woolworth's, so he's been staying home looking after the kids with measles. Switched on the TV, fell asleep in the chair. The wife had lit an untrimmed oil heater in the kids' bedroom. Dad didn't check it, probably hadn't been near them for a couple of hours—they didn't scream loud enough! It's all out of proportion, though.''

''What is?''

''Talking as a policeman, Ted, how often would you say that the punishment fits the crime? For the rest of his life that man will feel he committed double infanticide. For the time being he's blaming the government and the fire brigade. Next week he'll hit the bottle a bit harder, trying to be his own judge and jury.''

Hendricks said, callously, ''You're being very philosophical today, Alan.''

Alan drained his glass and pushed it back. "Yeah. If you want to change the subject, Sergeant, it's going to cost you. I'll have another."

When Hendricks came back, he said, "No Lennie, yet. I led a small posse down the river this morning to see his father. Took us an hour to locate him. He's a character, isn't he? Scrub him up a bit, and you could put him straight on a comedy show. I couldn't make up my mind if he'd seen Lennie or not."

"It matters?"

"I suppose Lennie wouldn't have had some crazy idea that his old man would ship him to the continent?"

"It's quite a trip from Benfleet to France."

"I have the impression that Henry Larkins was trying to hide something."

"Yeah. Himself."

"The Essex police are flatfooting it around your old village. Salt Lea."

"Go on?"

"You don't sound interested, Alan. Understandable. By the way when were you last back there?"

"Back?"

"At Salt Lea. The cottage is still standing, isn't it?"

"Salt Lea hasn't been bombed since nineteen forty-two."

"Sentimental journey, perhaps?"

"I'm not the sentimental type."

"I did wonder if Lennie might have gone into hiding there."

"Yes, he might. Not that Lennie's sentimental either."

"There was this place he called his cave. In the old quarry, wasn't it?"

"How did you find out about that?"

"A mile outside the village? Overgrown by woodland,

46

now. Your brother—sorry half brother—Gordon mentioned it.''

''You've had a busy morning, Sergeant.''

''We went to Essex via Norbury. Can be done.''

''You didn't call at his bank!''

''As a matter of fact, yes.''

''That makes my day! Who did you pretend to be—Henry Ford, Jr.''

''Come again? Look, Alan, I hope you haven't got that motor bike of yours with you.''

The brasses on the beams of the saloon bar were beginning to go into orbit. ''That's how you people do it, is it? Inject people with double whiskies, then go out and make them take a breath test.''

''It's Friday, Alan. My superintendent is having kittens. I told you, he doesn't like the public overreacting. Little girls told not to go picking buttercups in the park for instance, in case they come across the Big Bad Wolf. He wants action.''

''Aren't you action enough?''

''Tell you what I was going to ask you. Who's Aunt Val?''

Bombshell! Suddenly Alan thought he knew what Shirley had been trying to tell him—or, rather, *not* tell him. The usual Bishop noninvolvement, of course.

Bits of truth were oozing into Alan's hazy brain, now—things he'd long forgotten as well as all the things he could never forget. Like the smoke after an explosion . . . But he wasn't bleating it all out to Hendricks, at least not yet. He had to think first. Alone. And he wanted to listen to the other side of that cassette.

How the hell had Hendricks found out about Aunt Val?

Alan clutched his glass too tightly and said, ''Oh, Aunt Val.''

"Yes, that the name that's cropped up. Reckon she's just a figment of Lennie's distorted imagination? Like Uncle Ross?"

A second blast! Alan said, "Yes . . . when we were kids we did know them, vaguely."

"How vaguely?"

"All kids have people they take a fancy to, haven't they? Even Lennie."

"They weren't actual relations?"

"No."

"They lived in Salt Lea?"

"Yes." Alan's first deliberate lie. "But they moved away years ago."

When Hendricks didn't pounce at once, he hurried on. "I take it you got Doctor Zutmeyer to part with his confidential case notes. How did you do it—extract a few fingernails?"

Hendricks grinned, unpeeling one of his little cigars. "The eminent doctor was rather upset to find one of his cassettes missing. I immediately had a theory about that, but I wasn't prepared to be any more cooperative with him than he was with me. Don't make a habit of that sort of thing, though. You could grow into the best one-handed pickpocket in the business. Heard it yet?"

"Some."

"And?"

"Just a lot of gibberish—Lennie complaining about the hospital."

"Luckily, there's a secretary who types up the interviews from the cassettes. If you haven't heard it all, old lad, perhaps you should. And if it gives you any ideas, let me know. Had enough of that poison?"

"Yes, thanks!"

"Well, I must be off. We've got a dart game at the station. Then I'll have to catch up on my psychology. Lennie symbolizes, I think the term is. For example, when he refers to a 'red star' what's he talking about? Something just floating about in his brain? And there's something even more puzzling. Where the hell would Lennie, when he was a kid, have seen airplanes take off from Salt Lea? So far as we can discover, the nearest runways were at Southend Airport. I see I've given you a lot to think about, old lad. Weren't those bits on the cassette you pinched?''

Alan watched Hendricks open the swing door, not looking back. He pushed his glass away without bothering—or daring—to finish it.

He thought: Why not just stick to Maggie Jones, Sergeant? Isn't her corpse enough?

After all, who were Aunt Val and Uncle Ross, except ghosts from the past?

Only Lennie, as usual, had done the haunting.

chapter 6

Alan hoped that Mrs. Friday would be out shopping or devoting her solicitous attentions to a sick relative.

No such luck. He had just reached his room when he heard her slippers on the stairs. She knocked, opened the door, pilloried Alan with her eyes and said, "Where were you last night? Out on a job?"

"Yes."

"We're in a bit of a muddle here. Electricity's gone wrong. Fuse, I expect. Just in case you wanted a bath or anything."

"No, thanks. I've only come by for some papers."

"They work you round the clock don't they? Will you be in for tea?"

"I'm not sure," said Alan.

"What about this murder then? They're after some loony who escaped from a hospital over Brixton way. A youth, they called him—didn't give his name. I suppose you know all this."

"Who, me?" smiled Alan. "They leave that sort of case to the dailies."

"Well, sorry about the hot water."

Alan waited until Mrs. Friday's slippers had whispered down the stairs, then fed the cassette into his own recorder.

There had obviously been a break somewhere. By now Lennie was on a different track.

Doctor Zutmeyer: "What sort of trouble, Lennie?"

"The rabbits and birds and that."

"You got into trouble over rabbits and birds?"

The flat tone was the same: "It was these kids. They was always hanging around, see needling me like."

"Where, at your Aunt Val's?"

"Well, not at her house. It was on my holidays, though. I found this place with the airplane in it. There was a hole around the back where I got in. I fell asleep on some sacks. There were rats in there. You could see them staring. They never bothered me, though. Not like these kids. You could always shoot the rats."

"Shoot, Lennie?"

"Yeah. Like I done the rabbits and birds."

"Where did you get the gun?"

"My Uncle Ross give it me, didn't he? He taught me to shoot. He had lots of guns. He never minded if I took one of his guns."

"In this place, Lennie, the place with the airplane in it . . . You stayed out there all night?"

"Well, Aunt Val didn't mind, did she?"

"And Uncle Ross?"

"Well, he wasn't there, much. He taught me to shoot, you know? He had this beat-up old jeep. We used to go out on the marshes, shooting, like, and sometimes he give me boat rides. Once I shot a rabbit."

"Did you, Lennie?"

"It was running. Running toward the bushes. I had my gun. I just aimed and pulled the trigger. It didn't run no more." Lennie's characteristic snigger. "I ran and picked it up by its hind legs. It was all sort of warm and quivering, and its guts was starting to come out. It wasn't dead, though. I had to fire the second barrel to finish it off."

"Took it home for dinner, did you Lennie?"

"No. My dad said it was no good."

"Your *dad*, Lennie?"

"It was all shot to bits, he said. He picked up what was left of it and flung it in the hedge. His dog fancied it but my dad wouldn't let him touch it. He let off at me—said I shouldn't have shot it twice. But I had to put it out of its misery, didn't I? Maybe I should have just bashed its head in with the butt."

"How did you feel about the rabbit, Lennie?

"It was trying to crawl off with its guts coming out. That's why I fired the second barrel."

"The place with the airplane in it, Lennie, and the rats. You shot the rats did you?"

"Yeah. Well, she started shouting at me, didn't she? Called me crazy and things like that. She didn't know the gun was real, till I pulled the trigger."

"That was not far from your Aunt Val's, was it Lennie?"

"Not all that far. Anyway, I could find it easy even on a dark night. There was this red star, see? All I had to do was follow the red star. Then I went back to my mom's. She never even asked me where I'd been. Soft, my mom is. When I get out of here that's where I'm going. Back to my mom's. I mean, what good am I doing here? Lousy place, this hospital. Lousy food and the lousy nurses are at you all the time. Yesterday, this guard called McBride, know what he did? He picked on me. They're always picking on me . . ."

Alan pressed the forward button a little way, then farther and farther. Lennie was still complaining about the nurse. This occupied the rest of the tape. There was nothing more.

Alan stared at the machine, trying to shake off the aftereffects of Hendricks' whisky. Then he played the cassette through again, and again.

It brought the memories ghosting back, but proved nothing. With Lennie there was so little distinction between dream and waking, true and false, today and yesterday—or, for that matter, a street in Streatham or a desert on Pluto!

But not so fast. Suppose Aunt Val, and perhaps Uncle Ross, were still *there?*

Alan's editor-in-chief had a penchant for old American movies. He glanced up at Alan from beneath his Edward G. Robinson eyeshade and said, "Yes, of course I shall respect your confidence. I'm sorry, Alan. So you're wanting some compassionate leave? Well, let me see . . ."

He rummaged about among his scattered papers. "Difficult to spare you. Cummings has just fallen off his bike, silly young fool. However, I dare say we'll manage. We've got a new young fellow joining us this afternoon, temporarily of course. Jimmy something. I did his headmaster a favor some time ago. I should have known better. Now he thinks he's doing me one! As you may remember, I'm a great believer in the dictum that the first thing to do with a budding journalist is, somehow, to stop him from writing! Well, good luck."

Alan's exhausts crackled on the way to the Dartford tunnel. He imagined a sort of protest in that crisp, twin note as if even they were asking where the hell they were going and why.

He thought he could hit the Essex estuary in about an hour or less. Whimsically, he glanced occasionally into one of his twin mirrors, wondering if Hendricks were having him tailed.

Smart or not, what could Hendricks know of the turmoil in his mind? Alan didn't know, either. This was a journey in search of answers.

On the other side of the river he hit the A13 weaving past

heavy trucks on the way to Tilbury docks. Then the traffic cleared a bit.

Alan had been uncertain where to go first and to whom. For some reason, Mrs. Bishop drew the short straw.

The first thing he noticed was that his mother's blowsiness had practically vanished as if she'd undergone a face lift. The small hotel had a vacant, out of season air. There was the smell of fresh paint. Two women sat drinking coffee in the entrance lounge, so his mother took Alan through to the bar which had recently been closed. "Drink?"

"No, thanks. I'm not staying long."

Mrs. Bishop poured herself a gin. "Got some news, have you? I don't know if I want to hear it or not."

"Lennie? No. There's no news yet."

Relief or indifference? Mrs. Bishop nodded inconsequentially at the small raised rostrum against one cherry red wall. Through the casement windows there was a view of a distant silver sea and a deserted shore. "We're going to have a little band here this season. Frank's idea. You've not met Frank?"

"No."

"He's out seeing a builder. We've got trouble with the guttering. He'll be back soon."

Alan said, "You seem to be doing all right, Mom."

"I'm not complaining."

She'd run out of small talk. She said, "Don't tell me it crossed your mind that Lennie might be here?"

"Not really."

"All I know is what I've read in the papers. He won't, Alan, but if Lennie does turn up here, you know what we'll do, don't you?"

"Yeah?"

"Frank and I. Frank won't put up with any nonsense from Lennie. We'll just get the police and have him sent back to the hospital. They should never have let him out."

54

"He escaped."

"But they *do* let him out. Sometimes. Let's hope this time they'll lock him up for keeps."

Alan said, "Where's Henry Larkins?"

"What do you want him for? And how should I know? If the booze hasn't got him yet, I suppose he's still out on the beach, Benfleet way."

She was not hostile, exactly. There wasn't enough feeling for that. Alan found himself thinking, you spawned Lennie, you and that old layabout. What gives you the right to shrug off all the responsibility, drowning the past like an unwanted cat?

The man came into the bar, a large square figure in overalls, thinning gray hair, purple jowls, eyes narrowed on them both. Alan's mother said, "This is Alan, Frank. He just dropped by."

"Alan? Oh, Alan!" He shook hands perfunctorily. Then he turned away and helped himself to a drink from one of the bottles over the bar. He said casually to his wife, ignoring Alan, "They say they can do it next Tuesday. Let's hope we don't get too much more of this damned rain."

"I'll be off," said Alan.

Frank came from behind the bar and saw him to the door. "Nice to meet you, Alan. Always welcome here, you know. Come and stay with us sometime. Mind you, it gets busy in season. We're packed solid till autumn. We put on a good show at Christmas, though. Ten pounds a head and a free half bottle of wine to go with it. Bring your girl friend."

"Thanks," said Alan.

He looked back, but his mother had already turned away and was washing the glasses.

There couldn't, decided Alan, be many more desolate places than this one in the south of England. He bumped his bike as far as he could toward the rim of the estuary. He ditched it at the top of the brow, afraid that otherwise he'd rip his tires to pieces on the sharp shells of the beach.

The tide was still a long way out. A few small, scattered boats leaned in the mud, tethered to rusty chains. The distant water was a silver mirror, with gulls swooping down, then screeching away as if startled by their own reflections. Other birds stalked the shore, scavenging the tide's leavings.

The old motor cruiser was on its side, held there by winch chains. Because Alan was the only figure in view, Henry Larkins glanced up at the sound of his feet on breaking shells then looked back at what he was doing.

He did a double take, recognizing something that was familiar behind Alan's untidy beard, and said, "You're young Alan Bishop."

"Hello, Henry. How are things with you?"

"Could be worse."

He was not so old as he appeared at first glance—or so drunk or perhaps so stupid. Alan sensed that his arrival had not been quite a surprise.

Henry was using a sharp tool to scrape the timbers. "Barnacles," he said. "Damn nuisance, barnacles." He chipped away for a full half minute before he gave up and met Alan's eyes. "Don't tell me you're looking for Lennie as well?"

"As well?"

"Had a cop around, Sergeant somebody. Slippery character; treated me like he thought I was smuggling illegal immigrants. It was him told me about Lennie. First I'd heard of it. Where do you fit in?"

"Just asking around. Nobody seems to have expected him to duck the police this long."

Henry Larkins placed his tool carefully on the bow of the boat and fished out a can of tobacco. "He ain't altogether crazy, you know, is Lennie. Was it you who put the police on me?"

56

"Not intentionally."

"Who, then? Your mother? Never mind. It don't matter. I haven't set eyes on Lennie—not for years. I thought they'd locked him up for keeps. As for my boat, it's been beached for over a week."

For some reason they both looked across the flat sea to the faint and spare coastline across the estuary under the bright afternoon sky.

Henry Larkins said, "Want a piece of advice, son? Why come down here after Lennie? That's the law's job, isn't it? If he's dropped out of sight like the rotten apple he always was, what's it to any of us? Maybe he did that girl in, and maybe he didn't. The next guy who comes down here asking my opinion I'm going to clout with a marine spike."

"I see what you mean," said Alan with a grin.

Henry relit his stub of cigarette. "You can bleed to death, caring for Lennie. And you can lose a lot of sleep remembering things best forgotten." He went on in an apparent *non sequitur*. "Do you know, I nearly married your mother once? Must have needed my brains tested even to think of it. She promised to change her ways. Luckily for me, as it turned out, she two-timed me, so I married a boat instead! She did her best to get me back, you know. Even shoved a court order on me over Lennie. Just think, I'd have found myself trying to bring you up. All shapes and sizes and colors. Not me, mate. All right, so I'm a selfish old bastard. Tell you just one more thing."

"Sure," said Alan. He had to wait while Henry got the tip of his tool under one of the barnacles and prised it loose.

"I've always thought she conned me, your mother. I don't have to prove it any more, but I never reckoned Lennie *was* my son."

Alan hesitated. "Do you know what became of Uncle Ross?"

The eyes wouldn't quite meet Alan's. "Ross? Why do you

ask that? The answer, son, is no—and I care even less. He let me down over the business. Still, I've forgiven him by now.''

"And Aunt Val?"

"Oh, her. She could still be around, somewhere. I did hear she'd given up the post office." His eyes fell on the coastline again. "You've asked enough, son. So far as I'm concerned, the past is a different universe. Neither you nor the police are going to make me talk about it. See you, then. Even if it's only at somebody's funeral!"

The Suzuki took Alan, without too much protest, to Salt Lea, three miles away and farther inland.

A sentimental journey? No Sergeant, not that!

He hadn't been sure how he would feel, seeing Salt Lea again. Now he knew. Nothing. He felt nothing. It was like glancing at some old photograph of no special importance.

Alan killed his engine at the start of a muddy street. They'd built a short row of new shops: a newsstand, a grocery, a third shop, which was still empty with a To Let stuck slanting across a plate-glass window smudged with fresh putty.

The Norman church tower stood close by with its cluster of mossy tombstones. There was a bus shelter. How long had buses taken the trouble to travel this far?

Alan propped the bike on the stand, took off his helmet and wandered along. As he approached the old cottages he felt a sort of nostalgia that had little to do with either remembered happiness or any sense of belonging. The houses were simply there, much as they'd remained unimportantly in his mind, like a picture which you hung on an empty wall.

At number nine an upstairs dormer window stood open with bright scarlet curtains flapping like tongues. The short, front garden had become immaculate under a stranger's hand.

58

But the stranger had kept the gate. The only difference was a coat of pretentious silver lacquer.

Alan stared too long at it. There was the flutter of a curtain in the downstairs window. A woman's head appeared through the glass: inquisitive, mutely questioning, waiting . . .

Alan turned away and collected his Suzuki.

A last short journey, along another muddy path toward a rim of trees. He abandoned his bike and wandered down the slope.

The quarry was there. No policemen, no dogs. In the end, he didn't even bother to scramble down into the forgotten tunnels.

He got astride his bike again and bumped his way to the main road.

On the A13 he sometimes reached eighty and was back in Clapham inside the hour.

chapter 7

Sally wouldn't be at home—she had a pottery class right after school. Alan needed to wash up, if the fuse had been fixed, and he might as well have tea.

He hadn't been in his room longer than ten minutes when there was a tap on his door. Alan opened it, and there stood Hendricks. "I told your landlady I was from your insurance agency and that we had an appointment. Got a minute?"

"How did you know I was here?"

"Saw your bike outside."

Hendricks didn't wait to be invited but peeled off his raincoat and flung it on the back of a chair. "They told me at your newspaper that you'd taken the afternoon off."

"I don't have any beer, Sergeant. Cup of tea?"

"Thanks very much." His eyes swam ironically after Alan as he went to the corner and filled the electric kettle. "How did your little trip to Essex go today?"

"So you *did* have me tailed!"

"Good lord, have *you* tailed, Alan, with gasoline the price it is? We'd have had to borrow a super-charged Jaguar from the advanced driving school. There are more economical ways of finding out what goes on."

"Such as a hot line to the Essex police?"

"Well, perhaps you need your muffler seen to, old lad. Down there in Salt Lea, for instance, I gather they thought

60

they were being opened fire on by an offshore Russian cruiser.''

"So you know I didn't bring Lennie back on my pillion.''

"You expected to? Your mother . . . glad to see you, was she?''

"You had the hotel lobby bugged?''

"Did you meet Frank?''

"Yes, I met him.''

Hendricks grinned. "I bet you don't know he's got a record.''

Alan put the tea bags into the cups. "Go on?''

"Not important. Some years ago and petty stuff at that. Society's forgiven him by now. Surprising, though, they seem to have had so little trouble getting a license for that hotel. In your mother's name, before she married, I suppose.''

"Either that or Frank's gone so straight he's joined the local Round Table!''

"What sort of reception did you get?''

"They invited me down for Christmas—at my own expense.''

"You had a chat with Henry Larkins, too, didn't you? That boat of his interests me.''

"You've got him worried there, Sergeant. He thinks you're trying to bust him for smuggling in foreigners.''

"Really? The plot thickens. My experience is that when people get apprehensive about imminent arrest it often means they've done it. That old tub of his isn't everybody's idea of a luxury yacht, but it would have quite a range.''

"So Frank Haines is an ex-con, and Henry may be a smuggler. Sugar?''

"Spoon and a half, thanks. No joy at your old village then?''

"It's not been a particularly joyful day.''

Alan poured, and Hendricks looked on with that glassy intensity of his. "Clever the things you can do with that hand, Alan. Sorry. I suppose I'm being personal."

"Who, *you* Sergeant?"

"I wonder why you took up newspaper work? It says a great deal for your character."

"Good or bad?"

"Setting out to be a journalist, even with the help of that little gadget of yours must have been quite a challenge. Don't you guys aspire to something like a hundred and forty words a minute in shorthand, or am I going back to Lord Macaulay? Then there's all the typing. It wasn't an obvious choice of profession, was it?"

"No," said Alan. "But there was a surplus, at the time, of one-handed pianists. I thought we were talking about Lennie."

"Oh, we are. We are indeed. I suppose it's occurred to you that at this very moment, wherever he is, Lennie could be taking potshots with his little gun at God knows what or who? Suppose he kills again, Alan?"

"Again?"

"You can't have forgotten poor Maggie Jones—if he did it. I don't want to abuse your hospitality, but I wish you'd stop playing games with me. You're not particularly good at it. I'm only taking you on for old time's sake, like playing my seven-year-old at cricket and letting him win sometimes."

Alan laughed. "Games? *What* games, Sergeant? If you want to know, I was trying to help. Honest citizen and all that. You don't think I'd cover for Lennie?"

"You might," said Hendricks, adding obscurely, "in certain circumstances. You haven't asked how I knew about Lennie's gun."

"Doctor Zutmeyer's transcripts, of course."

62

"Yes. I got through a hundred pages of Lennie's spiel this morning with the script propped on my bathroom shelf while I was shaving. No problem. The shooting bit was on the cassette, was it?"

"It was you, Sergeant, who suggested that Lennie symbolizes. The gun's probably about as real as his mysterious red star."

"Mysterious?" asked Hendricks. "That reminds me. I'll have to hoof it back to that hospital. Better step carefully, though. I have the feeling that Doctor Zutmeyer has an ax to grind."

"He doesn't want bad publicity for his hospital or to have his precious theories torn apart. Anyway, I thought the idea was that we all wanted Lennie back fast, without too much trouble."

"You haven't, I suppose, remembered where Aunt Val and Uncle Ross lived—exactly, I mean?"

"No. I hardly knew them." Another lie.

"A surname would help."

"Sorry. I told you, they weren't relatives, just people who took a passing interest in Lennie. What do they have to do with anything?"

"Probably nothing. We're just trying to check on everybody—everybody who might be harboring Lennie. We're beginning to run out of addresses. Oh, well, Essex is a big, sprawling county. It has to *be* Essex, of course?"

"Where else?"

Hendricks sipped his tea, then said, "Tell you something, Alan? You Bishops puzzle me. Apart from you—I think I'm right—none of them cares whether Lennie is found, dead or alive. There could be, I tell myself, some sort of a conspiracy—not to shield Lennie, but to protect vested interests. Pride, guilt? A need to forget? I wish I knew that. Shirley? She played it dumb like we were members of the vice squad.

Gordon? I thought he was going to threaten to write to the commissioner. Lennie's father? Spat tobacco and seemed to think we'd invented Lennie as some mysterious means of parting him from his boat. Your mother—Lennie's mother?—offered us a drink out of hours, queened it up a bit, made a point of mentioning that Royalty had almost booked in there, once. Frank isn't quite family, is he? He's simply got the idea that our main object in life is to persecute the ex-prisoner. For some reason, you're the one who's really jumping about on a hot tin roof over Lennie. I wonder why?"

Alan said, "Some of us, Sergeant, do have a sense of responsibility—even for a half brother. And for people like Maggie Jones."

"Yes," agreed Hendricks. "Fair enough. But why *you*, old lad? Why not Gordon, for instance? It doesn't make sense, you doing all the leg work for the family—even if you have got a pair of wheels! Thanks for the tea. I'll be in touch. Will you be at Sally's tonight?"

Alan flushed. "Maybe."

"Good!" He turned at the door. "Oh, by the way, Lennie may be in the clear regarding Maggie Jones. Just a detail. There was a coat covering part of her body—it got mislaid, somehow, by the time we arrived on the scene. Temporarily, that is. A zip-up waterproof jacket—no significant markings. Wasn't the sort of thing Lennie would have brought from the hospital, though. The lab's checking it, just in case it tells us anything."

It hadn't even rung a small bell with Alan, at first. He'd got through his burned kipper downstairs and was trimming his face in the bathroom before it hit him.

Shirley had said, *"I even gave him a zip-up jacket that was lying around."*

It wasn't important to conjecture why Lennie, if the coat

was the same, had taken it off and used it as a shroud for Maggie Jones. He'd long ago stopped asking himself silly questions about Lennie.

Alan thought of ringing Shirley and warning her; how long would it take Hendricks to put two and two together, go to the apartment and confront her with the jacket? But there had been no "significant markings" (why did Hendricks tell him so much that he didn't need to?). And Shirley, frankly selfish, detesting the fuzz, knowing nothing would bring Maggie back, not wanting to be involved, would deny all knowledge. Fair enough—did it matter?

Yes, it mattered to Alan. That long ago they had all covered for Lennie—all except Shirley, who hadn't been around. Alan, Gordon, Mrs. Bishop—even old Henry Larkins. And others . . . Lay off, Sergeant! Why drag them back into Lennie's slime?

Lennie had killed—and they'd known it! Hendricks: *"There could be, I tell myself, some sort of a conspiracy—not to shield Lennie, but to protect vested interests. Pride, guilt? A need to forget?"*

Too right, Sergeant! Take your pick. But, you see, it's not just poor Maggie Jones. You half know that, don't you?

And it had seemed all right. (*"Gordon and I were only kids, Sergeant."* A good excuse?) Lennie put away, responds to treatment and has no history of serious violence since. But if he *did* choke Maggie . . . we were wrong, weren't we?

Terribly wrong!

But I'm the one left with all the guilt, Sergeant. Why me?

A glance at his own face in the mirror—a face like Lennie's. And some new truth was grimacing back, trying to tell him something. *What,* for Christ's sake?

Alan hadn't planned to go on a binge.

He rode his Suzuki to Sally's, but instead of going up he parked the bike out of sight and found a pub.

Quiet enough. Alan downed a whole pint and felt better—or did he mean worse? Not too slowly the alcohol opened the pores of memory.

Uncle Ross: *"Come on, boy, you can do better than that. The thing you've got stuck under your chin is what they call the butt. Pull the trigger and you'll knock off your head! Tuck it against your shoulder, firm. That's better, and mind where you're pointing the muzzle. Jeeze, it scares hell out of me watching a left-handed kid hold a gun. A bit of practice and you could switch. Trouble is, you've got your left eye on the sights. That's okay if you happen to be left-eyed as well as left-handed, but I've never known a left-handed shot yet who didn't spray his grandmother's arse at ten yards."*

A big, shambling man was Uncle Ross, smelling of old tweeds and beer and tobacco. Voice like a tree saw. There was the trudge of heavy boots in the wet, then the sudden silence. A long silence, broken only by breath in his nostrils and the sudden lift of a massive, unshaven chin with a deep cleft. Pale, wide-spaced eyes gazed through dew-dripping trees and then . . . the fall of a hand on Alan's shoulder, unexpectedly light and affectionate, a hand which somehow claimed him?

Alan went to replenish his glass for the third time. The man behind the bar said, "How old are you son?"

"Eighty-two."

"Don't give me that lip. Just say eighteen and I won't argue."

"Stuff it!" said Alan.

The second pub he went to was called the Golden Cock. An accommodating barmaid gave him a single whisky. "How much soda?"

"Quite a bit, thanks."

It didn't help.

Aunt Val said, *"I can't hide him all the time. I can't*

66

watch him all the time. He just comes and goes, you see, Alan? I do my best. Sometimes I think he's tucked up safely in bed, and when I go in he's gone."

"It's not your fault, Aunt Val."

"He's so gentle. He's gentle with Smokey. His hands are soft, Alan, so soft. I was going to get in touch . . ."

"But you didn't, Aunt Val. Ross told us, but not soon enough."

"What good would it have done? Even if he did it, you can't bring the dead back, can you? Take him home, Alan, then they won't know. Nobody will know . . ."

"It's not as easy as that, Aunt Val."

"You're so bitter, Alan. You hate him, don't you? Because he broke your hand in the gate . . ."

"I saw the gate yesterday, Aunt Val. They've painted it silver. It's no longer the same gate. No bits of bone. That's the difference, isn't it? Between the inanimate and the living. You can paint a gate, an iron gate, and it passes at once into a different time. No scars, no bits of flesh. It's only the living that go on living."

The pain . . . never such pain. Lennie must have worked it out to the second. Alan's wrist was in the right place, idly, thoughtlessly, wrapped around the iron post. There was no reason for it. They'd been playing ball in the front garden.

Lennie came, giggling, raised a leg, planted the sole of his shoe on the gate and slammed it shut. When Alan screamed, Lennie giggled.

The doctor at the clinic had said, "A great pity he wasn't brought in at once, Mrs. Bishop, we might have been able to do more."

"I was out—on business. I didn't know."

"I'm afraid the tendons and nerves are badly damaged. The X rays show serious multiple fractures. We'll do all we can, of course. An accident, you said?"

"Of course. The boys were fooling about. You know how it is . . . He won't lose the use of his hand, will he?"

"We must just hope for the best. It is his left hand."

"But he's left-handed . . ."

The bar was getting crowded. Somebody put the juke box on. Alan got up, lumbered to the door, felt air on his face.

And finally he found the Eagle Tavern.

Plush, well appointed, mirrors on the walls in elegant silver lacquer frames.

That face again, Lennie's face. He thought he could smell one of Hendricks' little cigars. *"Who's Aunt Val, Alan? And Uncle Ross?"*

"I don't remember. We were only kids at the time."

"They lived at Salt Lea?"

"Not really. Anyway, Uncle, Ross traveled around quite a bit."

"Had some sort of business deal with old Henry Larkins?"

"Yeah."

"So Uncle Ross would have known your mother and Aunt Val?"

"He knew a lot of people."

"Why did he take so much interest in you, Alan? You and Lennie?"

"I don't know."

"Come off it. You can do better than that. He taught you both to shoot."

"And to play tiddlywinks!"

"Uncle Ross was your dad, wasn't he? And Lennie's. Only you had different mothers."

"No wonder you're pushing for inspector!"

"But it makes a difference, doesn't it? Now I see! Lennie isn't Gordon's half brother, or Shirley's. He's all yours,

68

Alan. Is that why you care so much? Do you love him or hate him, Alan?

"You mean . . . there's a difference?"

"Get Lennie for us, Alan."

"Why the hell should I, Sergeant? You said yourself, he's mine. You're a smart detective, but it'll take you at least a week to find out where he is. I could do it tonight."

"You won't, though, will you, old lad? And suppose you did?"

Alan reeled to the bar and, somehow, back. The mirrors were full of people.

"So you fancy yourself a crime reporter, Bish?"

"Well, he's found himself a brother, hasn't he?"

"Yeah, and a real live poppa, too, haven't you Bish?"

"Nice cover job you did on Lennie, Bish. What are you going to do next, blow his brains out?"

"Who, Bish? He wouldn't pull the legs off a spider."

"Don't you believe it. Still waters run deep."

"Better start swimming, Bish. Get at the truth, man."

"Didn't some guy say the truth will make you free?"

"Yeah. Jesus Christ. You've got one up on him, though, haven't you, Bish? You're going to kill Lennie. That makes you God Almighty!"

Sally said, "Alan, you're drunk!"

"Yeah."

"Something's happened?"

"Lennie didn't kill Maggie Jones, did he?" Alan muttered. "They're wrong about the coat."

"You need some coffee—black. And lots of it."

chapter 8

Alan said, "It's a fallacy that coffee helps. It's just another stomach irritant."

"It's not your stomach I'm concerned with," Sally said. "If you want to be sick, you know where the bathroom is."

"Do I detect a note of disapproval?"

"You do! Not because you're stinko, but because you got that way alone. Next time, take me along."

"I wouldn't have been very jolly company . . . No fresh news, is there?"

"About Lennie? No."

"Sally . . . I want to talk, if I can stumble over the consonants. I don't think Ted is the sort of cop who would grill his little sister under a five-hundred-watt bulb. So I'll give you practically everything, in my best, crisp journalese. It's got to be that way with us. I warn you, though, I've hardly had a coherent thought since Thursday morning."

She curled up close to Alan on the settee. "I'm listening."

"Honey, I'm scared! And very confused. I think I know where Lennie is—with his mother. And he's been there before, those other times he's been missing . . ."

"His mother! But I thought . . ."

"No, not Mrs. Bishop. She just fostered him. When we were kids, there was Aunt Val. A sweet, simple sort of person, a bit harmlessly crazy herself. She was always very kind to me, but she was especially fond of Lennie. Naturally! Not that I gave it any thought at the time. There was also a character we knew as Uncle Ross . . .''

"Lennie's father? Not your old Henry Larkins?''

"There, I told you! If I'd filled you with half a dozen gins and tonics you'd not have been so quick on the uptake. Yes, I think he was Lennie's dad. I believe he's mine, too. Uncle Ross was quite a guy, if you like that sort of fellow. Someday I'll tell you about him."

"Yours too?''

Alan shrugged. "He moved around a lot. He knew . . . my mother. It isn't important, not now, but you see, if it's true, then I'm Lennie's half brother. That makes him my responsibility—or am I being insufferably old fashioned?''

Sally lit a rare cigarette and puffed at it, like a child. "No. But go on."

"Lennie was eleven. He killed someone—a girl—with a gun. We all covered for him. Very clever, we Bishops! The police never found the killer. They thought it was an accident, I guess. Anyway, we got away with it. So did Lennie, of course, only—mainly because of Gordon—he was sent to an institution. A few months later . . .''

"After . . . what he did to your hand?''

"That was part of it. Does it matter?''

"Yes!''

"Never mind. It was because I was *me,* you see? Not Gordon. Not anybody else. *I* was his half brother. You'd have thought he knew! I was like him, especially then, and perhaps he did know. But, coming to the present, Maggie Jones . . .''

"Ted doesn't seem to think he did it.''

"*I* do!''

"On the way in you said something about a coat?''

"Yes.''

"And?''

"I think it was one that Shirley gave Lennie."

"But they—the police—won't be able to prove it?"

Alan gulped at his coffee. "I ought to tell him, of course. Ted, I mean."

Sally suddenly got up and crossed to the record player. She put on a disc.

Alan said, "Mozart."

"Yes."

"The Requiem Mass. Very appropriate!"

"I'm sorry. I didn't think . . ."

"Leave it!"

"You've been through hell, haven't you?" Sally said after a moment. "So you don't want Lennie found?"

"Oh, yes."

"Then why . . . ?"

"He's mine. Your brother told me—I think. If I'm not tearing down there this minute and strapping him to my pillion, that's mainly because I wouldn't be able to keep the police out of it. They—probably not Ted—would pick up my exhaust smoke and pounce, plod around that village, tear everything apart, zoom in on poor Aunt Val. She doesn't deserve that. Isn't it enough, being Lennie's mother, without having her name plastered all over the papers as a witch who's given birth to a killer?"

Sally said, "But Alan, you can't think of everybody."

"I can damn well try!"

"Sweetheart, you're taking far too much on yourself."

"Am I?"

"You're afraid—because the police know this?"

"Yeah. It's all in Lennie's dossier. I caught a bit of it on that tape. The gun, the place . . . only no names."

"What place? You said a village."

"That's the only thing I'm not telling you."

"Not Essex?"

"I didn't say that!"

"But he's sure to be found."

"Yes. But not yet!"

"So what are you going to do?"

"Who me? Put him out of his misery, maybe, like he did with a rabbit!"

Sally dismissed the latter. She said, "Alan, there's a point of law called, I think, conspiracy to defeat the course of justice."

"Justice? Didn't somebody say the law was an ass?"

"Dickens. Does this music depress you?"

"No. Here's my credo: life ought to be simple, built on faith."

"Your consonants are doing quite well."

"Thanks. The trouble, now, is I feel wide awake. Somebody else once said consciousness was a biological accident. Suppose Ted calls again?"

"For me—or for you? I never think of him as a detective. He's still just my big brother." She gave Alan a long look. "What are you doing to do next?"

"I'll fetch Lennie—if he's where I think he is. I told you, he's all mine, now. I'll get him back to the hospital and his one, true friend, Doctor Zutmeyer. If, as I think, he killed Maggie, that's out of my control. If he didn't, well, the past is past. Nobody's going to rake *that* up if I can help it."

Sally stroked his face. "Mind if I say *my* piece?"

"Go ahead."

"You care too much—whether from love or hate—and that's made you feel like God. But a primitive god, Alan— something that speaks through the thunder, not from a cross."

"So Lennie should be allowed to crucify us all?"

"No. Not that. But I think you've got yourself in quite a muddle, Alan. You can't even really hate Lennie, not deep down. It's not that simple. Yes, of course one can hate a brother. But something else, something more important, gets in the way. A sort of caring. Gordon doesn't care about Lennie. He just doesn't want him turning up at the bank one morning and getting in the way of his promotion—after all, it turns out he's barely related. It's different for you, Alan. You've half admitted it yourself. *You* care. In a way, you're behaving like a child—because of what you've learned.''

"Oh, thanks!''

"You think you care about Lennie's mother too. Well, you do, but it's Lennie you're really chained to. Symbiosis, to use a technical term.''

"Symbi-*what?*''

"Love is partly possession, a means of self-identity. A temptation to power—over another's life—perhaps even his death.''

"Thanks for warning me!''

"Did I ever tell you about Starkey?''

"Starkey?''

"He was the class cat, a stray, actually. He turned up one morning, out of nowhere. He was just a kitten then. My class of six-year-olds adopted him. He'd spend most of the day curled up on some little lap, and we took turns giving him milk, and one of the kids even spent his pocket money on a can of cat food.

"He couldn't be kept in the classroom all day, of course, but he'd always come back, growing fatter and more dignified. In the end you'd think he owned the school! Well, one day there was an incident in the playground. I was a little late on the scene because I was wiping somebody's bloody nose in the cloakroom. When I got out there, just about every child in the class was over in the far corner by the fence. Over the tops of their heads I saw a flash of blue and yellow trying to peck its way through the wire mesh. And there was Starkey.

74

"It was somebody's escaped parakeet. The kids didn't know to whom it belonged, and Starkey was trying to get the bird. Do you know what the kids were doing?"

"I can't wait!"

"They were belting Starkey—with sticks! They'd picked up sticks and were beating that cat. If I hadn't intervened in time, they'd have hammered it to a pulp. Why, Alan? Because they loathed Starkey, all of a sudden? Because they loved the parakeet? Not at all. They'd never set eyes on it in their lives. You see, they were mostly about six years old, and they were still groping toward the dichotomy between love on the one hand and nature being red in tooth and claw on the other. I tried to tell them about it afterward, about cats wanting to eat pretty birds, but it cut no ice. They looked at me with open mouths and dazed expressions as if I was some sort of monster. Perhaps some of them did grasp the simple concept that cats *do* eat birds, but Starkey wasn't just a cat, you see? He was Starkey—just as Lennie is Lennie, your brother. And they expected him to behave in a way that— well, that just wasn't natural to him."

"To hell with marrying you," Alan said. "I'd do better with Sophocles."

"Give me your hand, Alan."

He gave Sally his right hand.

She laughed and said, "There! I've caught you out. Do you realize that you always give me your *right* hand? You're a bit thick sometimes, honey. Don't you know it's your *withered* hand I want?" She took hold of it. "Whatever you think you're going to do, it won't be tonight. I've got some sleeping pills somewhere. A souvenir of the last school inspection.

The telephone purred, pitching itself in competition with the dawn chorus of birds out on the common. Sally crawled out to answer it. She came back. "For you, Alan. Ted."

"Oh, hell!"

"You'd better talk to him."

Alan got to the phone. "Yeah?"

"Sorry to disturb you, old lad. Something's come up. The lab's just got around to that coat."

"Coat?"

"The one the killer used to cover Maggie's body, remember? There's blood on the collar. Lennie's group. Not conclusive but suggestive."

"So?"

"So I want you here, Alan. On the double, eh? At the station. I'll be waiting. And I'll want to hear it all, you understand? I mean *all*."

Alan was still pulling his clothes on when Sally appeared. "They want you—at the station?"

"You've been eavesdropping."

"Trouble?"

"You could say that. Lennie *did* kill Maggie."

"Oh, Alan!"

"See you, eh?"

"Yes, when you get back."

Alan kissed her tenderly. "Don't believe everything you hear, honey. Just remember what I told you. Lennie's mine. He's my charity of the month. But my so-called family isn't going to escape its share of the responsibility this time." He headed for the door. "If I don't arrive at Gestapo headquarters, tell Ted I got a blown gasket—anything you like."

chapter 9

Shirley looked a mess and knew it. "Has that blasted motor bike of yours got insomnia? What time is it?"

"About half-past six."

"Hell, boy, I didn't know there was such a time! Coffee?"

"If you're making it."

She vanished into the kitchenette, then came out, banged a few cushions into place, emptied a couple of ashtrays. In the early morning light she looked shriveled and almost child-like.

"Okay, let's have it. On the phone you said something about a coat." She didn't wait for an immediate answer. Her voice continued from the kitchen. "All I got is canned milk, okay?"

"Sure."

She came back with two coffee cups, which she placed unsteadily on a low table stained with the rings of vanished glasses. Sitting opposite Alan, she carefully draped her dressing gown over her knees before she asked, "What about it?"

Alan felt irritated and jumpy. It was the hangover, partly. "I'm surprised you haven't had an early morning call already. They've found Lennie's blood on the collar."

Her eyes flashed. "You mean the little reptile has real blood in his veins after all? Yeah . . . he must have cut himself shaving. Shaving! I remember now. He said he wanted a shave, don't ask me why. I let him borrow a razor. What did it matter to me if all he had on his face were pimples?'' She laughed, suddenly.

Alan asked, ''This is funny?''

''Yeah, well, it's that coat. The guy who left it behind was having a night out on the town with the boys. He'd ditched his wife in a hotel around the corner. If they trace the coat back to him . . .''

''They won't,'' said Alan. ''They'll probably ask you, though, why you withheld evidence.''

Shirley's eyes went blank. ''Did I? Listen, so far as the police are concerned there never was any damn coat. Not one I knew anything about.'' Then the new horror struck her. ''Jeeze, so our Lennie did kill her! I never really believed it, you· know?''

''Our Lennie?'' asked Alan.

Shirley read his face. ''You've got things on your mind. Want to unload them?''

''Lennie's with Aunt Val. She's his mother.''

''You telling or asking? Okay, yeah. That's what I figured. I nearly told you, remember?''

''But you won't tell the police that, will you? Where Lennie is, I mean.''

''I get it! You're trying to pull a fast one on the fuzz yourself. *Now* who's withholding evidence? And why? What's in it for you?''

''Nothing. It's just . . . Well, for one thing, I don't want Aunt Val hurt again.''

''And for another?''

Alan chose his words carefully. ''Something happened . . . years ago, when we were kids. It's suddenly occurred to me that you probably don't know about it. You'd left home by then.''

78

Shirley lit a cigarette. "Something Lennie did?"

"Yes."

"And you don't want the police raking it all over with their little pitchforks?"

"You *do* know!"

"I didn't say that. When can I go back to bed?"

"Have you ever been in touch with Aunt Val—since she gave up the post office, I mean?"

"Yeah, I went down there to see her, just the once. It was years ago, though. I stayed for tea. I stroked her cat, Smokey. I told her I'd got this swell job as a receptionist at London Airport."

"And she told you . . . ?"

"Nothing, boy. You remember Aunt Val? Sweet as sugar, but her conversation floated about all over the place. I put one or two bits together, that was all. You, Lennie, Gordon . . . It didn't make a lot of sense. And I still don't want to know the details. Anything else?"

"I need her address."

"Is that all? The cottage is called the Glen. It's about a quarter mile up Creek Road, on the left. Okay?"

"Yeah, thanks. Shirley . . . Uncle Ross."

"You got around to him too?"

"So you did know him?"

"He was around, on and off."

"Tell me about him."

"Big, tall guy. Worked with old Henry Larkins. Gee, did he fancy himself! Strutted about like he was Paul Newman in a Western."

"It sounds as if you knew him pretty well."

"He made a pass at me—more than once. I was only around eleven at the time. Maybe if I met him now . . ."

"He lived at the old lodge?"

"Yeah, but he could bed down pretty near any place.

Sometimes he camped out. You know how it is with guys like him.''

"Sometimes he stayed with Aunt Val?''

Her eyes danced. "Unless it was all done by remote control! Uncle Ross played the field. What the hell has that to do with anything?''

"You wouldn't know where he is now?''

"Who, Ross? Dead or in jail maybe or married and settled down in Australia with six kids. Does it matter?''

"And sometimes he stayed . . . with our mother?''

"Oh, Mrs. Bishop!'' Shirley lit a second cigarette. "You won't leave anything alone, will you? That's your problem, boy. What does it all matter? You hung up about your dad? Not me. You think I care whether mine was a dock hand or the ambassador from Tanzania?''

Alan grinned bleakly.

"What are ancestors but a lot of old, dry bones?'' Shirley continued. "If you want me to spell it out, maybe you'd better have a shot of brandy in that coffee.''

"No, thanks.''

"I was around six when Lennie was born, right? Gordon was already toddling about, mapping out his future and collecting pennies in a box. Then, suddenly, there was Lennie.''

"Suddenly?''

"Gordon wasn't the only precocious baby in the family. Even at that age, I knew something was crazy. *Mrs. Bishop wasn't pregnant!*''

"So?''

"So Lennie was a bouncing baby in the crib. He was a month old, at least.''

"You wouldn't have guessed who Lennie's real mother was.''

"Not then. I worked it out much later. Aunt Val was a respectable postmistress and her figure was like a dried-up twig.''

Alan asked, ''When did you guess that Uncle Ross was my father?''

''When I watched you and Lennie play together—if you could call it that. Always together. Alike as two fat little peas in a pod. You were such a honey with him, Alan. Even when he got into a tantrum and bashed hell out of you—nearly always you, hardly ever Gordon—you'd always forgive him and totter back for more of the same treatment. Real little brothers, weren't you? This is partly hindsight, I know. But somewhere along the line it hit me. The crazy bastard isn't *my* brother or Gordon's. You think I feel any different, now? He's *yours,* baby—all yours!''

Despite the preliminary phone call, Gordon was annoyed. When Alan arrived he answered the front door himself but didn't ask Alan in. He said, ''I've got to pop into the bank for a couple of hours. Auditors down from the main office. We'll talk in the garage. Don't want to disturb Angela. She's just gone off to sleep again after your phone call. Seven o'clock was a bit early, wasn't it?''

''Sorry,'' said Alan. ''I'm taking a certain course of action and . . . I wanted to see you first.''

''Action?''

Gordon slid back his new electric garage door. They sat in the front of the car looking through a polished windshield at the blossoming rhododendrons in the front garden.

Alan said, ''I thought it was only fair to warn you.''

''What about, for goodness sake?''

''There's going to be trouble, over Lennie.''

''I don't see why I should be involved.''

''Don't you?''

81

"It's Maggie Jones that matters, isn't it? They're not going to dig back . . . to the other time. Even then I knew it was wrong."

"You mean, what we did? Are you claiming it was my idea and I dragged you along by force?"

"I didn't say that."

"There's a pretty bright detective on my back."

"Oh, you mean Sergeant Hendricks. I thought he was some sort of friend of yours."

Alan laughed. "If you've got a friend like Hendricks, you don't need enemies! He's up for inspector. Someone higher up has given him his head."

Gordon winced. "If you ask me, Alan, it's probably your own fault. He's hammering away at what he regards as your weaknesses. You just can't help opening your mouth, can you, and giving yourself away? Why not be out when he calls?"

"I'm sure you were cleverer when he interviewed you."

"It's not a matter of cleverness, Alan. It simply pays to play dumb with the police. Mind you, they're there to do their job like anybody else, but they need cooperation don't they? Talking of jobs, why aren't you trotting around interviewing the aggrieved public or whatever you do for that newspaper?"

"I've taken some leave."

"What the hell for? And why drag me in?"

"So far I've kept you out of it."

"Kept me out of what? My conscience is perfectly clear. We gave Lennie the benefit of the doubt. All we did was rig him out with a little alibi. I'm not saying we didn't need our heads examined, but after all we were wet behind the ears. There's no possible connection between *that* and this murder—unless you oblige the police by handing them one on a plate."

82

"Aren't you being a bit complacent?"

"Yes. I'm a complacent sort of chap. I find it pays. *You* should try and cultivate some complacency yourself."

Gordon reached for a duster and began meticulously wiping the inside of the windshield.

Alan said, "I've learned a few things I didn't know before."

"Such as?"

"Lennie's not your half brother—only mine."

"I've often wondered. Sorry, but I'm rather glad to have it confirmed at last."

"Our mother . . . fostered him."

Gordon raised his eyebrows. "Good lord, are you saying he was Aunt Val's brat? Well, well! Yes, it makes sense—of a kind. Our dear mother had one virtue at least. She liked babies. Not children, babies. Once we'd shed our diapers she tended to lose interest, don't you think? That's why she let Lennie run loose. That's why when he smashed your hand in that gate it was twenty-four hours before she got around to taking you to the emergency clinic. I can still hear your screams, Alan. She'd have been a wow as Mother Goose, wouldn't she? Hatching us out and listening to us go tweet-tweet. So Lennie was a sort of cuckoo in the nest!" Gordon glanced at his watch. "I'm due at the bank in ten minutes. If you don't want an unnecessary ride, you'd better come to the point."

"I suppose it's stupid to ask you for help."

"Doing what?"

"Getting a day off. Coming with me to fetch Lennie."

"No, I wouldn't say you were stupid, Alan. On the other hand, I don't quite see your problem. If you think you know where Lennie is, go and get him. I don't see how all three of us could squat on your Japanese bike! Ring your friend, Detective Sergeant Hendricks, and give him the lowdown. All they'd have to do is buzz down in their Black Maria, or whatever, and pick Lennie up. What's the problem?''

"I have tried to tell you."

"Melodrama, old boy. If you're right, Lennie's sitting in his mommy's parlor right now, feeding his nasty face with cornflakes and cream. Aunt Val will be doing what she no doubt always did. Pat Lennie's head, tell him to be a good boy, and not go shooting rabbits, unless Uncle Ross is around to make sure he doesn't aim too straight! Silly, irresponsible old woman!''

"You could be wrong, Gordon, about some things."

"Yes? Well, I really must be going. I still don't understand why you bothered to come here this morning at the crack of dawn."

"I told you. I need help."

"What are you expecting to achieve? It's not even as though Lennie, in this enlightened world, will come out of it too badly, whatever he's done. He'll probably go back to the hospital, get an extra slice of bread and jam for tea and, of course, in due time another weekend pass so that they can unload him on one of us and cut down on their food bills! As for help, as you call it, I'm very busy. It's Saturday, and this afternoon I'm thinking of pruning my roses. Look here, old boy, if you insist on sitting there you're going to have to walk all the way back from the bank.''

Alan hesitated only briefly over his choice of routes. Lennie, he told himself, would keep for a few more hours. And if the police wanted to follow him into Essex, that was their privilege!

He reached Southend by midmorning. He didn't go to the hotel but found a telephone booth. Some handyman answered, and it was two ten-pence pieces later before Mrs. Bishop got on the line.

"Why don't you come here? Where are you?"

Alan told her.

"You on your bike? You're only about three minutes away."

"I'd rather meet somewhere else, if you can spare the time."

"If it's Frank you don't want to meet, he's out. I'm rather busy getting the lunches ready. Well, all right. Where do you suggest?"

"Regents Hotel—coffee shop. You know it?"

"Of course I know it. As a matter of fact, Frank and I are thinking of buying it!"

Alan hung up. She was there in about a quarter of an hour. She was dressed quietly and respectably in a light tweed suit and a pair of horn-rimmed glasses. Her hair had been kept tinted in her favorite auburn, and she had a neatly coiffured set of waves executed, no doubt, by an expensive local hairdresser.

Alan beckoned a waitress. His mother said, "This is quite nice. They could do with a fresh coat of paint, though. Look, I mustn't make it too long. One thing I've learned in taking on a hotel is that the minute you're out of sight everything goes wrong. What do you want to talk about?"

"Aunt Val, for a start."

She seemed mildly surprised. "Why Aunt Val, for goodness sake?"

"I think Lennie may be with her."

"You've a reason for thinking that?"

"Yes . . . She's his mother."

Alan hadn't been sure how she'd react. Nothing spectacular. She poured coffee and asked, "How did you find out?"

"Did it have to be such a big secret?"

"No. I just never got around to telling you. It didn't seem . . . important."

"What was?"

Her eyes glinted behind her glasses, conveying a new hostility she didn't yet comprehend. Then she said, composedly, "Before we go any further, shall we get one thing straight? I did more for Lennie and the rest of you than you'll ever know. I'm not saying I was the perfect mother—who is? But who do you think brought you all up—the Virgin Mary? Who fed and clothed you and changed your diapers? And dragged myself along to all your schools, where everybody would be icy polite and call me *Mrs.* Bishop. 'A bright lad you've got there, *Mrs.* Bishop.' 'Let me see, *Mrs.* Bishop, your little girl is adopted, of course.' "

"Who says we're ungrateful for all that?" Alan shrugged. "Perhaps I needn't have troubled you. It just felt . . . important to hear it all from you. About Lennie, and other things."

"Make it quick."

"The guy we called Uncle Ross. He was Lennie's father—and mine?"

She took that coolly enough. People were coming into the coffee shop. She patted her hair and put on a fixed, conventional smile which had no connection with anything. "How did you make the great discovery?" she asked. "All right, yes, he was your father. At least I'm almost certain he was. You could have done worse. Ross was quite a man, in his way."

"Aunt Val thought so too?"

The smile stayed. She said, "Val came to me one day and told me, 'I'm pregnant, Eileen.' I was surprised she even knew the word."

"What did you suggest? An abortion?"

"You younger generation! No, I didn't. I said she wasn't to worry. She could have the baby, if she wanted. Out there, hardly anyone would notice. She had help in running the post office. Funny thing is, she was happy, poor cow! When the time came, she more or less planted Lennie on my doorstep. I suppose you got most of this from Shirley.''

''Yeah.''

''Little tramp!''

''Isn't that making insulting remarks about a kettle?''

''Watch your tongue, sonny!''

''Sorry! I'm on my way to fetch Lennie. I wanted to know the score first.''

''You're a bit off the track, aren't you?''

''It depends.''

''And why? Haven't you ever grown out of feeling responsible for Lennie? You're his half brother, not his keeper, for God's sake. After the things he did to you . . .''

''Somebody has to . . . bother.''

Still the polite smile. ''You're a smug little fellow, aren't you? What makes you think you can get there before the police?''

''They're concentrating on the wrong district. They can't have found out, not in detail, about . . . the other thing. Not yet.''

Her face hardened. ''Listen, Alan, as I told you before, keep me out of it. I did my bit all those years ago for Val's sake—not any more. There's something you should learn—growing older is like kicking away ladders and clinging tight to what comes next. There's no way back.''

''Aren't there some ladders you *can't* kick away? Uncle Ross isn't still around, I suppose.''

''No, of course not. He went abroad years ago, so I heard.'' She nodded at a passing acquaintance, put her smile back on and said, ''Val used to refer to Ross as Mr. Steadman. Always Mr. Steadman! Hell, she was simple. Do you want to know anything else?''

''Do you ever see her?''

"No, why should I?"

"Just another ladder, is she? Like Lennie."

Mrs. Bishop got up, opened her handbag and left a pound note on the table. "Remember, Alan, whatever happens, don't involve Frank and me in all this. It's got nothing to do with us. Since you've chosen to stick your nose in, Lennie's your problem. Understand?"

chapter 10

For too long the sky had been the dome of his own head. Back astride his Suzuki, however, Alan shot a brief look at the real thing. Black silver-rimmed clouds rushed across the heavens, as if he were accelerating in a time machine.

There was no view of the sea from here, but the beat and rush of it sounded, in the distance, like a plague of starved gulls.

Was the tide in yet? Alan hadn't noticed. When he left the shelter of the town, he cut his speed because the wind across the beach road threatened to blow him off course.

It was after noon, and Henry Larkins was probably holed up in a pub somewhere. And the tide was a long, long way out. Then he found a little inn, quaint, "olde worlde," with a thatched roof and a pair of white-painted wagon wheels nailed to the porch.

The menu featured sandwiches and omelettes. The proprietor had a bald head, sidewhiskers and a cheery, eighteenth-century mine-host manner.

Alan inquired, "When is high tide this week?"

"Around two—I think. I don't remember exactly."

There was a scatter of other customers, mostly in turtleneck sweaters, one sporting a battered peaked cap. He overheard and chipped in, "Two forty-three, by the book. It's usually on time!"

A couple of men laughed. One looked up, his eyes full of beer. "Wanting to hire a boat, son? For fishing? Not today, you don't—unless you got waterwings! I wouldn't go out there in a submarine in this weather."

Alan grinned and carried his lunch to an empty table beside a leaded window. He found himself counting the heavy droplets of sudden, blown rain.

What goes on, Bish? he wondered. Why the relief? You're supposed to be feeling frustrated, eager to get on with it. Find Lennie, don't sit around killing time.

Various complications struck him—one, there was no *proof* that Lennie was with his mother. Two, there was even less guarantee that Lennie would come quietly. What was Alan going to do—put a rope around his neck and drag him off to catch a train? He wouldn't have his bike with him, and Pebblemarsh didn't have a station. Three, he ought to call Hendricks or somebody. He even found himself counting how many ten-pence pieces he had.

Four. He felt scared. The sweat was coming back—he was scared to hell!

Alan spun the time out, getting his pipe going, nursing a second half pint. When he finally left the pub the rain had stopped, and he thought the wind was slackening. He rode the mile or so back and left his Suzuki chained to a fence beside a half-demolished building, helmet looped over the saddle. Then he went in search of the steps down to the beach. Henry Larkins was there now. He had his boat tilted up the right way, its name visible in flaking paint on the bows: *The Sea Queen.*

Henry was farther up the beach, working his rusty winch. Alan sneaked up behind him and grabbed the handle.

Henry Larkins apparently thought he had just miraculously received divine assistance. Then he turned, sheltering against the rush of water and wind. *"You* again? Let's keep her heaved to, son. She's in a channel. It took me an hour to get her on keel. Been working on the engine all morning. I was going to test it, but I don't fancy this weather. There! That's got it. If you want to talk, you'd better come aboard."

Alan followed him, clambering wetly into the cockpit behind the shelter of the windshield. Henry squinted disagreeably. Apparently he couldn't get the windshield wiper to work. "If you're wanting a trip, you'd better leave it till tomorrow. Reckon I'll call it a day."

"I'll make it worth your while."

Henry Larkins squatted down and rolled one of his inevitable cigarettes. He was no fool, and in the last twenty-four hours his brain had probably worked overtime. "What can you give me that I can't do without? There's still half a gale blowing out there."

"I bet it was worse at Dunkirk."

"Yeah, but I was nineteen at the time, and I thought I was Christopher Columbus. You reckoning on finding Lennie—across in Pebblemarsh?"

"So you've worked that out?"

"Not all of it. Why do you think he's with Val?"

"She's his mother."

Henry's dentures clicked. "Go on? You sure?"

"I'm sure."

Then Henry did a double take. "Hey, that means . . ."

"You coughed up that bit of maintenance for nothing, Henry! Unless . . ."

"What, me and Val? You're joking, son! Listen, are you trying to duck the law over this? You're figuring that if I give you a lift they'll think you've gone off and drowned yourself? Whatever you got in your head right now, boy, it ain't brains. That detective sergeant—he'll know what happened as clear as if we'd made a film of it. And who'll get the blame? Me—Henry Larkins. What's more, the river police come out as far as this sometimes.''

But he was beaten, and knew it. ''One thing for sure, Alan, it'll be a one-way ticket. Don't ask my help in bringing Lennie back.''

Alan shook his head. Henry went on, ''Last time it was you and Gordon and me. You know what we should have done then, don't you? Dumped Lennie over the side, with a spare anchor tied around his neck.''

''We live and learn.''

Henry Larkins dropped his spent cigarette over the side and pressed the starter. The old boat throbbed into motion. Alan dangled his Suzuki keys, ''There's just another small favor, Henry. I parked my bike in the village—you'll find it. If there's some way you can get it under cover for me I'd be grateful. Chucking a tarpaulin over it will do for now.''

Henry peered ahead. ''So long as you don't want me to ride it somewhere. When do you fancy you'll be back?''

''I don't know.''

''Well, if it's after opening time, don't come bothering me. I'll be at some place inland getting drunk—celebrating!''

The shore across the water had a different kind of bleakness. The tide had ebbed again, and it was necessary for Alan to clamber up a flight of green, slippery steps in order to reach the jetty.

The beach showed no signs of human life. The skeleton of an old dinghy was sketched near the water's edge and beyond that were only bits of rubbish and crops of stones crowded with screeching and pecking birds.

The skyline behind Alan looked remote and deceptively abandoned. In the distance there were squat, alien shapes of oil refineries and other installations. A single row of pylons

92

bestraddled the almost treeless landscape. More birds chirped on their sagging wires.

There was a gap in the barbed-wire fence, giving access to a narrow, twisting roadway. The village of Pebblemarsh lay half a mile farther along. Nobody, nothing passed Alan on the way as he headed toward it, almost on tiptoe, as if in this quiet place even his footsteps might alert a malicious presence concealing itself in the scrub.

There was silence in the village. A little church with a spire of broken tiles marked the village center, and bungalows were dotted here and there, half concealing themselves at the ends of muddy paths.

The sub post office was no longer there or, rather, it had been converted into a cottage with white stucco walls.

The telephone booth had survived. Alan wondered whether Aunt Val would have a phone, but he had no idea of her number, and when he went in to look through the directory he found that some bored adolescent had ripped it to pieces. It didn't occur to him to call the operator.

He came out and ran smack into Hendricks. The sergeant had drawn his car up outside the booth, patiently waiting for Alan to emerge. He was driving his own private unobtrusive Ford; muddied tires, engine running. Alone, of course, he was smirking through a foggy side window, which he eventually rolled down. "Hi, there, Alan. What have you done with your motor bike? Want a lift?"

There seemed no point in trying to get away. Alan walked around the car and got in beside Hendricks, who said, "So you're coming quietly?"

"Where?"

"Fasten your seat belt, there's a good chap."

"I might want to make a break for it."

"Back to Salt Lea? It's a long swim."

Hendricks drove off. It was some moments before he said,

"This is a godforsaken place, isn't it? I wonder what it's like on Sundays."

Alan didn't trouble to answer. His eyes were fixed without interest on the flat gray estuary. Occasional vessels crept in from the sea, accompanied by barking pilot boats worrying them into their prescribed channels. Eventually Hendricks said, "You're not asking what I'm doing here, Alan. Not admiring the scenery, I assure you."

"You've always managed the answers without my bothering to ask the questions, Sergeant."

"It's all quite simple, in a complicated sort of way. This is still supposed to be unofficial. Partly my super's idea, of course. He's only human, and when it comes to the unorthodox he has a way of winking at you—or rather, twitching an eyebrow. If the idea works out, he takes the credit. If it doesn't, somebody else is sure to get the blame. In this case, I suppose, if anything goes wrong he'll fix it with the chief constable down here. I'm not sure even to what extent he thinks I'm involved in this business—at a personal level, I mean. Sometimes I have the feeling he suspects me of boring a few holes in a crate and shipping Lennie to Honolulu. As you know, he's got that all wrong. Anyway, here I am. Hendricks, private eye, wearing out his own tires, acting incognito. I'm exceeding orders, not daring to tread on anybody else's toes. If it works, maybe I'll get my stripes. If it doesn't . . . Say, this damned road doesn't seem to be leading anywhere."

"You're in the driver's seat, Sergeant."

"I had quite a problem with your Aunt Val, Alan. You see, I didn't have a surname. And was she Miss, or Mrs.? Was Val a pet name or short for Valerie? Still, I asked around and eventually hit the jackpot. By the way, I saw Lennie."

"You *what?*"

94

"Helping in the front garden! Being a good boy, for the moment. Why the astonishment, Alan? I'm sure you didn't hitch a rough ride in Henry's old boat just for the sea air. He didn't offer to give you a bit of moral support, did he?"

"No."

"Or Gordon or your mother? Frank might have been useful."

Alan laughed. He said, with no particular relevance, "Mrs. Bishop used to have her own way of handling Lennie. She'd drag him upstairs by the scruff of his neck. Then, when she'd got him to the top, she'd throw him down again. Could be quite effective, when Lennie was around three."

"Not much family rapport, then?"

Alan said, bitterly, "You thought we'd all come down here like a band of brothers, storming the ramparts? My mother, Sergeant, expressed it very well: she's kicked away ladders, the ladders back to the past."

Hendricks abruptly swung off the road and cut his motor. "Ah, the past, old lad. I was coming to that."

"I thought we were just going to sit here watching the ships."

Hendricks drummed on the steering wheel. "It'll be an early dusk. I think Lennie will keep till the sun sets. Better if it isn't done out of doors, at the front of the house, with the neighbors having a grandstand view. It was very providential, Alan, your turning up when you did. I thought I'd have to slip into another of my disguises and play a bit part as a male nurse from the hospital." Hendricks seemed to be talking to himself, now, pale eyes on a huge cargo vessel plowing its way up the channel. "I take it you'd still prefer to get Lennie yourself?"

"Yes."

"Well, go easy. He probably won't have completely forgotten that he choked Maggie Jones on Wednesday night.

95

Anybody turning up suddenly will represent a threat. It's getting chilly, isn't it?''

He got the car moving again and slowly retraced the stretch of deserted sea road the way they'd come. There was no more talk until he'd stopped yet again, pulling into the entrance to a farm, facing a five-barred gate. From this spot they had a clear view across country. A row of pylons bestraddled newly sown fields and marshland. A couple of hundred yards away stood the gaunt shape of a large, square building, black against the cloudy sky.

Hendricks said, no longer tauntingly, ''Remember *that,* Alan? Used to be an airplane hangar—belonged to a firm that made agricultural machinery. The directors had a light aircraft which they used to flip across to the Continent on business—maybe spend a little of the shareholders' money on vacations in the south of France, for all I know. No wonder the firm went bust! The place is just a barn, now.

''Speaking of vacations, that's what Lennie called them, isn't it? The times he spent here with his mother—your Aunt Val. And, on and off, Uncle Ross, of course. She let him run loose a bit, didn't she, in the old days? He'd camp out in the hangar somehow, like he did in the quarry across in Salt Lea. And he never got lost in the dark because, apart from his sense of direction, he'd worked it out that all he had to do, when he wanted his bed and supper, was follow the line of navigation lights on the tops of those pylons. Let me see . . . Yes, the fourth in the line from here is close enough to what was the post office in Pebblemarsh.

''It was all rather elaborate, of course,'' Hendricks continued, ''but then Lennie has a strange mind. Another confusing aspect is that in his chats with Doctor Zutmeyer he sometimes refers to more recent visits to his mother's new cottage. That doesn't matter.

''Alan, just now you referred to your family as kicking

away ladders. But you've a ladder too, haven't you, old lad? Anyway, you're at the top, looking down—all the way down to a night in May, 1970, just seven years ago. Lennie was—what—eleven or so? You a couple of years older? Gordon would have been around fifteen. Shirley had already left for London, hadn't she?''

Hendricks turned to Alan for confirmation, but Alan merely sat there expressionless, looking straight ahead. "I told you," Hendricks said, "I've been chatting around and looking up the records. There was a little girl who was reported missing—a bit older than you, at the time. Her name was Rebecca Bryant. It took them two days to find her. She was half hidden under a pile of old leaves in a copse, not a stone's throw from that barn—the hangar, as it then was. Not a pretty sight, apparently. She'd been killed at close range with a shotgun.

"Now, the local police had problems. They did their best, but there was no clear evidence of murder. For one thing, she hadn't been sexually assaulted—and such missing girls usually are. That didn't rule out another child's having done it, of course, but what child would be in possession of a shotgun? The circumstances did tend to suggest that whoever killed her hadn't committed a deliberate crime—even the leaves could have been blown over the body by chance. It had been a windy week.

"But there were poachers around, Alan. Over there, just about where that seeding machine is clacking away, was private land then. Woods, mostly. Keep Out notices on every bough. But all sorts of people augmented their daily diet with illegal rabbits, even the occasional pheasant in season. It seemed more than possible that Rebecca had been shot by accident—she'd have been trespassing, too. Whoever did it might, or might not, have known what had happened to his latest blast of grapeshot.

"Of course, they called in a bit of local expertise. There was a well-known character, for instance, named Ross Steadman. Very helpful, very cooperative. Took the trouble to show the local police his guns, safely locked up in a cabinet at the lodge, where he lived part of the time. Perhaps he wanted to clear himself of any possible suspicion—or someone else? Anyway, there was an inquest, of course. Verdict—misadventure. Weeping parents in court. Case closed. Warning from the coroner—they must always say their piece, mustn't they?—about keeping kids out of forbidden territory."

Hendricks broke off. When Alan didn't say anything, he went on, gazing through his misty windshield. "Well, so much for the facts, Alan. The rest, I admit, is fanciful—I always did have too much imagination.

"That barn must have been close to the private woods. Remember Lennie and the rats? Rebecca Bryant might have been one of them. Some local gang of youngsters who saw Lennie, pursued him, teased him, followed him to the hangar. They had a leader, perhaps—a loud-mouthed kid who knew it all, said that Lennie's gun wasn't real. But he wasn't the one who got his face blown to pieces, was he? Later, he and the others would no doubt have guessed that 'that queer boy' had had something to do with it. But Rebecca had been on her own—gone in search of Lennie. Why? To tease? Because she was sorry for him? Who knows, now? At any rate, the kids would have kept quiet—they'd have had to own up to trespassing, otherwise. And even if they had spoken up, who takes any notice of kids?

"All guesswork, Alan. And suppose Lennie had been suspected? Who knew about his nocturnal wandering except poor Aunt Val, who was the village postmistress and went to chapel every Sunday? And Uncle Ross, of course—who'd shown the police his carefully oiled guns.

"Of course, it was Ross who took charge, wasn't it? Only he kept Aunt Val out of it. When the body was discovered, he got on the phone to Mrs. Bishop like she was the fire brigade. He wanted his kid Lennie out of there fast! And she roped in poor old Henry because she had a hold on him—because he thought he was Lennie's dad. And you were the one who could, most of the time, cope with Lennie. It wasn't all that different from the present, was it, Alan? Our mutual friend Doctor Zutmeyer, who knew there was something sinister in Lennie's past, got the same idea, asked *you* to bring him back. And I wouldn't mind betting that Gordon found himself pushed into that boat, too. What happened—was he sick over the side? Sorry—I'm pushing it too far. But how am I doing?"

"As well as could be expected, Sergeant. So when do I get the usual spiel—about anything I say may be taken down and used as evidence?"

Hendricks peered out at the darkening sky. "I think we'll move in soon. Sure you want to do it alone?"

"Yes."

"Well, I'll be pretending to change a wheel just down the road. Alan . . . seriously, except for Lennie you've nothing to worry about. Time, they say, is a great healer. In some cases it can also be a useful sweeper under carpets. My super's view—I think. There will be some sort of hearing, of course, and you'll be required to give evidence. But *in camera,* Alan. No publicity, no raking over old ashes. It has occurred to you that there's *no proof,* so far as I know, that Lennie killed that first time?"

Hendricks watched Alan fiddle with his pipe for a moment before starting the car. "All anybody wants, you see, Alan, is to make certain now that a gate swings on Lennie—forever."

chapter 11

Parted from Hendricks, finding the cottage in the failing light, Alan felt the creep of sweat against his back—and his self-doubt returned. Why was he doing this? That damn Hendricks—he shouldn't have left him!

As he pushed open the gate, he had a wild thought: perhaps Aunt Val was really *everybody's* mother! Shirley's, Gordon's, *his*. And Mrs. Bishop had been on the make, as usual, stuffing pillows against her belly on suitable occasions and bringing up her silly sister's unwanted brats at five pounds a head per week!

This is no joking matter, Bish, he told himself. Get on with it. Get up that newly weeded path and bang on the door.

Aunt Val had pulled aside a net curtain and was peering down the long path. Alan pretended he hadn't seen her face, lifted the tarnished knocker and let it drop just once. It must have been a full half minute before a light came on in the hallway and she opened the door.

Alan said, "Hello, Aunt Val." She tilted her face, staring in the half light. She had aged. She was a white-haired old woman, shriveled, short-sighted, mouth trembling, eyes afraid.

Alan tried a smile. "It's Alan, Auntie. Alan Bishop."

He thought he heard a movement at the back of the house. Footsteps? The squeak of a door?

Aunt Val seemed to gather her wits. "Good gracious—Alan! What a nice surprise. Come along in."

"I'd better take off my boots."

"Go into the front room when you're ready. I'll put the kettle on." She hurried through the hall, presumably to the kitchen.

The front room had a covered sofa and matching armchairs, old-fashioned castors embedded in a frayed carpet. Brocade curtains, hanging on a broken rail, were drawn across the bay window.

There was a marble fireplace with photographs in black frames—whose faces? Against the faded wallpaper hung a picture of the Battle of Waterloo. Alan remembered it from long ago. And the cat—an enormous half persian, charcoal gray—came out from somewhere, crossed the carpet and rubbed its head on Alan's shin. Alan stroked it and murmured, "Hello, Smokey."

In a corner cabinet behind a glass front were some shotguns. Alan got up quietly to take a closer look. The cabinet was unlocked. Two long-barreled guns hung on their securing straps from stout hooks. They were well kept, fresh oil shining on the barrels.

There was a *third* hook with a tell-tale shadow of exposed wallpaper in the perfect shape of a third gun. Alan slid open the drawer beneath and saw packages of ammunition stacked tidily in their cardboard boxes.

Then he heard Aunt Val's footsteps, closed the drawer hastily and returned to the sofa. She held a tray with two Wedgewood cups and saucers and a plate containing a large slice of fruit cake. Perfectly composed now, she sat opposite Alan, poured tea and talked as if they'd been together only yesterday. About the cottage, a leak she'd discovered in the roof, the trouble she'd had getting someone to present a reasonable estimate for termite treatment. Then she asked a question about Alan's career, and, "Do you often see Gordon? And how's Shirley?"

Alan tried to swallow a piece of cake before he brought himself to ask, "Aunt Val, where's Lennie?"

Her tone didn't change, only the expression in her eyes. A quick look away, but no hesitation in her voice. "Out on the marshes, with Mr. Steadman." Alan had almost forgotten how precarious the balance of her reason was. "They spend a lot of time together, you know. Mr. Steadman is very fond of Lennie. He takes good care of him when he's here. It's a pity you've missed them, Alan. They should be home before dark, unless they go to the lodge. But you can hear the jeep a mile away on the road."

Alan could only play it straight, all the way through. He was worried about the sound he had heard. Lennie . . . *had gone out?*

"Uncle Ross keeps his guns in good condition," Alan said.

Aunt Val's eyes darted to the cabinet. She spoke in the same flat, matter-of-fact tone. "Yes. He showed me how to clean them. I don't really like the things—they frighten me. Once, he took one of them to pieces. He showed me it was perfectly safe without bullets."

"Cartridges," said Alan, automatically. "There are still cartridges in the drawer."

She didn't seem to hear. "You used to go shooting with Mr. Steadman and Lennie, didn't you, Alan? He often asks after you."

"They ought to be kept locked up, Auntie."

"I do lock them up. The key's in the drawer."

"The one with the ammunition in it?"

She was answering his questions without anxiety or suspicion. "There's a key to that in another little drawer—the one next to where the bullets are."

102

"One of the guns is missing, Aunt Val."

"Mr. Steadman said Lennie could borrow it. Afterward, he found it near the hangar, you know, and took it back to the lodge."

"Afterward?"

It was the kind of madness which created a compelling image of sanity. There sat Aunt Val sipping her tea, a perfectly guileless and sensible creature, bent forward a little on her chair, the words themselves giving no clue to her irrational state.

Alan knew he must assume command now. "Auntie, I've come to take Lennie back."

Then it was as though her mind shifted into a different key, the second of two parallel realities. "Yes. Of course, Alan."

"To the hospital. They are . . . helping him there."

A sudden gleam of alarm. "You won't hurt him?"

"Hurt him Auntie?"

"He won't go to prison, will he?"

"No, Aunt Val. Not prison."

She became thoughtful, compliant. "We must make arrangements. You haven't a car? Mr. Steadman would take you in the jeep, but he's going abroad. He has a new job. Yes, that's it—going abroad. Last night I dreamed about a gun, Alan. Someone was holding a gun against my head . . . Why do you keep looking at the guns? You're not going to *hurt* Lennie!"

Tears came stealthily to her eyes, overflowing on her shiny cheeks, but the only sound was the faint rattle of her cup and saucer.

Alan waited as her thoughts whirled away into shadows like a purseful of counterfeit coins. Whatever she was thinking, now, she paid Alan no attention—even when he got up and went as casually as he could to the guns.

He said, "Tell you what, Auntie, I'll see if I can find them—on the marsh."

He picked the gun he remembered best, then stuffed what he hoped was the right ammunition into a pocket. When he went out into the hall, she didn't turn her head.

He grabbed his muddy boots from the porch, went through the hall and eased open the back door. He squeaked it shut behind him and walked in his socks to the broken gate.

No sound from the cottage—nobody in the second lane. He propped the gun against the ragged hedge and pulled on his boots. Then he fished for the ammunition and loaded both barrels.

Yes, the cartridges matched . . .

Lennie? He'd find him. Lennie would be waiting, somewhere. *Waiting?*

Alan had clean forgotten Hendricks.

It seemed a long trudge to the lodge. By the time he had reached it the last of the day was vanishing. He remembered the twisting path down the steep slope between trees etching weird, still shapes against the sky. The wind had exhausted itself, leaving behind a stark and timeless silence.

He soon found the old driveway and progressed slowly along it, his feet crunching faintly on the gritty surface, eyes searching for tire tracks.

Nothing, of course. The lodge lay just past the bend, between two banks of straggling ragwort. The old stone dwelling would still be there, wouldn't it? Albeit in a state of abandoned disrepair or occupied by someone else, perhaps? Someone who would stand in a renovated doorway and, in response to Alan's improvised inquiry, set him on the right road for the village?

No, not even that! All that remained was a charred shell, bits of broken walls sticking up through the weeds like upthrusts of natural stone. From somewhere came a rustling sound that made Alan instinctively raise his gun muzzle. But it was only a blackbird, startled in the process of pecking at lingering garbage.

Alan turned away at last, wishing more than ever that he'd never come back to this place. He mistrusted his emotions, that was the trouble. What became of you, Uncle Ross? My father, I mean. And do I care a damn?

As Alan trudged up the final slope toward the tree-covered brow, he saw a figure waiting up there—a figure with a gun, partially concealing itself among the hawthorns.

Mesmerized, Alan climbed toward it, called out to it. For a second, he expected Uncle Ross himself to break from his cover and slither down the slope toward him with a squelch of heavy boots.

But there was no word, no movement. Unguardedly, Alan climbed toward the hawthorns, trying with all his will to subdue the mad fancies that had his mind.

Uncle Ross was a ghost, but *this* was no ghost. Something backed away out of sight, leaving a trail of swinging branches and the crackle of feet on undergrowth.

Reason returned and with it the old sweat. Alan cocked both triggers of his shotgun and got down on his elbows and belly, lumping the heavy weapon beside him. He forgot he had cocked the triggers and that, with a single awkward twist of his hand, he could blow his own brains out.

Still the twigs cracked some way ahead up the slope. Then he suddenly saw the dark country straight ahead of him— they still switched on the lights at the tops of the pylons.

Which red star was Lennie following now?

The movements in the undergrowth had stopped. Had Lennie run off somewhere? Or was he lying close by, waiting for Alan, a fugitive become the hunter?

There came a different sound to Alan's right. From the

cover of a tree he peered down and saw the rubbish pit. Someone had either climbed or fallen into it. There was a clatter of cans, stones, bits of metal. If Lennie were down there he had abandoned caution, or there might be some new problem in his twisted mind. He had been heading for a road, perhaps, had blundered into the pit and now was pinned like an insect in a web.

There was a series of sobbing moans like those of a trapped animal, then the awful quiet again. Remembering about the gun now, and keeping the muzzle pointed away, Alan eased himself toward the edge of the pit. He thought he saw a white smudge of face peer back at him through a pile of twisted girders.

Alan said into the darkness, "Lennie?"

Then a fresh movement set off an avalanche of rubbish— and a gun blazed! The air close to Alan was full of humming wasps. He ducked away fast, the shot reverberated across the fields and, when it had faded, Alan heard Lennie climbing out.

He backed away into the trees again, but Lennie was not coming toward him. Somehow he'd hacked his way out of the pit and was making off toward the road beyond.

But he didn't run far. Alan had a fleeting glimpse of his shadow half crouched, the big gun in his hand a narrow strip of shadow. Then, abruptly, his footsteps died.

Lennie was somewhere in the thick hedge that bordered the road. Licking his wounds? No, not Lennie! Alan heard the unmistakable sound of a breech mechanism. Lennie had fired off both barrels—didn't he always?—and now he had to re-load.

Alan lay very still farther down the hedge, his chin practically touching the asphalt of the road. He eased his shotgun slowly, slowly, into position. So that's how it is, is it Lennie? But you're not the only one with one of our father's guns!

Alan hadn't been silent or invisible enough. Lennie let fly again, the deadly swarm of humming grapeshot stripping the leaves off the hedge above Alan's head. Even before the echoes died, Alan heard the scuffle of feet.

Not off and away down the road, but doubling back toward him!

Alan's heart somersaulted, and his right hand snatched too wildly for the trigger guard. One barrel went off and the charge whistled into space. The footsteps stopped—Lennie knew the score, now?

But he was there, desperately close, so close that Alan could pick up the sound of his breathing.

You're stupid, Lennie. You're not even bothering to keep your head down, are you? I can see your stupid, mad face gawking at me through the hedge. Point-blank range, *brother!*

Very, very slowly, Alan got the shotgun across from his right to his left so that the butt was hard against his left shoulder. The double barrels were propped awkwardly on his useless left hand, but the forefinger of his right crept along the butt until it found the second trigger.

For what seemed a century, Lennie's face was there, hanging in the hedge, glowing like a Chinese lantern. And you're going to *kill* him, Bish? Alan thought. Come off it!

Lennie's gun blazed first.

No pain to speak of. A stinging in the shoulder, the sound of voices in his head, a confusion of high red lights and low blue ones.

Then Alan found himself sitting upright under a short row of those twinkling blue stars.

Hendricks said, "For Christ's sake, Alan, who do you think you are? The sheriff of Domesday Creek?"

Alan asked, "He missed?"

"Not quite," said Hendricks. "I think you've got a pellet or two in your shoulder."

"Which one?"

"Left. Don't worry, old lad, it won't make your shorthand any worse than it already is. I've got an ambulance on tap—if they can find us. They'll soon fix you up."

"And Lennie?"

"You mean you care? We got him. Just in the nick of time. He was reaching for that second trigger."

"Got him?"

"No, not *that* way, Alan. Are you disappointed?"

Hendricks looked up. "Here comes the meat wagon. They'll probably keep you in the hospital overnight, Alan. Just a checkup, mostly on your brains! Be a good boy, and I'll use my influence to send a patrol car for Sally. She ought to have better things to do, but she may want to pop down to hold your hand!"

Alan sighed as the ambulance pulled to a stop, and Hendricks hurried over to it. So they had got Lennie; the gate had closed.